MEEK
STRENGTH

Ian Pannell

Meek Strength by Ian Pannell

This book is written to provide information and motivation to readers. It's purpose is not to render any type of psychological, legal, or professional advice of any kind. The content is the sole opinion and expression of the author, and not necessarily that of the publisher.

ISBN: 978-1-952617-57-7 (Paperback)
ISBN: 978-1-952617-58-4 (Hardback)
Printed in the United States of America.

Rustik Haws LLC
100 S. Ashley Drive, Suite 600
Tampa, FL 33602
https://www.rustikhaws.com/

PREFACE

I have spent the majority of my adult life trying to adjust and master my own attitudes and behaviors based on the circumstances I've found myself in. I've maintained an extreme passion about life and have rarely been afraid to try new things. I often sought God for occasional help, since I thought His Influence was better used for large problems. I have been relatively successful in my pursuits, so I thought, "why should God help me?" However, I'm thankful close family and thoughtful members of my community were praying for me, when I wasn't praying for myself.

In 2013, I started logging my personal experiences because the conditions I thought I heard whispered to me, as the Promise of God, were nowhere in sight. Was I missing something; or was my timing out of alignment with His? My goal, at the time, was to carefully observe my circumstances through the lenses of past and present situations to determine how I got to that space and time in my life. It was also to seek and observe *material* evidence that our tallest dream is the Promise of God, which was established before we were born. Initially, I chose thirteen weeks to monitor and capture experiences that occurred and were resolved by faith, as I managed three statewide businesses with the bulk of my savings gone. A barrage of unexpected familiarities challenged me, as I ran head-first into every one of them without realizing – I was not required to.

Throughout my thirteen week journey of self-discovery from August 18, 2013 to November 10, 2013, I was convinced that God has my life already worked out. According to The *Old Farmer's Almanac*, a season is comprised of 13 weeks.[1] In the Bible and in the Book of Ecclesiastes 3:1, it says, "*There is a time for everything, and a season for every activity under the heavens...*"[2] In my 13-week season, I opened my eyes, inner ear, and heart to receive everything God wanted me to have. Additionally, I recorded observations to describe and share what

---

[1] The Old Farmer's Almanac, First Day of Fall 2013: https://www.almanac.com/content/first-day-seasons

[2] New International Version (NIV), Ecclesiastes 3:1

I learned in "real time."

I've often been reminded along the way that the Bible contains all truths relevant to our lives in the beginning, relevant now and forever. This may be a surprise to those who, intimately, know me as a self-professed "humanist," or one who believes in a sort of naturalism, primarily, to govern thoughts and behaviors in this life. I thought since we live in a *material* world we should act and react in it with material principles. To me logic and rationalism were more suitable because Godly attitudes and behaviors weren't appropriate to survive in our "evil" world. Oh boy, was I wrong!

Very often in our lives we come to a certain place or fork in the road when we need to make an important decision. What I learned from these very complex experiences is that at each "fork" where there are at least two choices, there is one choice that is a true choice for us at the time.

When we choose a *path* for the wrong purpose, the Spirit will lead us to the appropriate place on the *path* that intersects with our true *path* if we are faithful enough. The Bible, explicitly, says to look for the Spirit of Truth whenever we need guidance. Even so, we agonize over decisions and often make the choice we want based on money, prestige, novelty, or other reasons. Moments like these are when I, normally, sought God's help, and when I made the decision, I was comfortable that it was the right one.

When I "conclusively" discovered that sometimes God leads us through the fire to mature our soul, I found the process astonishing and not good or bad, but refreshing at the moment it was over. Before I became aware of this perspective, I perceived moments like these as a sign from God that I was losing His favor. This outlook brought along feelings of fear, guilt, and doubt. These feelings do not originate from God.

In my early twenties, God seemed like He was so far away; a Great Spirit that only people like my grandfather worshipped daily and totally trusted. I knew God was the All Powerful Creator, but I didn't know how to fit Him into my daily life. I felt like I had so much more living to do in the *material* world and my ambition was not settled enough to involve God since I was out for *self*. Worshipping God all the time meant I had to do everything right, and I wasn't ready to do everything right.

I was still young and there were things I wanted to see and try but not outrageous things, just activities "church folks" might frown upon. Most, recently, I've realized that God wants to be actively involved in everything we do because we are individual expressions of Him in *material* form. In the *material* world, we must seek a natural balance in our *material* and *spiritual* pursuits to, fully, appreciate this life. God is available for every step we take. He has either active or passive involvement in our lives, but He is always there whether we are aware or not. He is All-Knowing and Ever-Present, and it is best if our intentions are good.

We exist in human form to learn and participate in the world to re-discover and fulfill God's Purpose for our lives. If we can believe and appreciate this, then we should also believe there is nothing in our world that would be an obstacle for us to accomplish His Purpose – except *ourselves*. What I found is that we are most happy and enthusiastic when we are on the *path* to pursuing our true purpose in this life. This is the reason we exist here in the first place. But if we are not happy often and not feeling enthusiastic about our lives, then we are not, currently, aligned with our true purpose. When we realize this we have "free will" to, humbly, ask God for His help getting us back on the path to finding our truth in the world we live in.

Through my recent experiences I, strongly, believe that we will never find our true purpose and sustainable happiness without submitting to God and requesting help. For those who choose not to believe this, I humbly remind that we all have experienced, at least one dramatic time, when the limits of our *material* strength were tested and we came up short.

During this extraordinary time, we knew we had a decision to make and either chose to continue doing the same things as usual, or we fell vulnerably to our knees and sought His Guidance. For those who haven't had a dramatic fall yet, always know God awaits you with healing, after you fall and skin your knee. In our material world, we choose to be happy or miserable based on our decisions. We will never find perpetual happiness (joy), meaning, strength, love, emotional balance, or true purpose without re-discovering God first. My premise is: when we experience the power of the sentiments above without a *spiritual* motive they are *materially* inspired and short-lived.

In this journal, I recount a short story about the awesome start I had in my early life and how I discovered in hindsight 20/20 that it had prepared me for what I was doing. I've always known deep inside that I had a specific purpose, but like many people I had no idea what it would be. I believe and have a little evidence that God knew us before we were born.

He preinstalled a kind of "software program" that activates in us at some point to pursue His Purpose for our lives. The Bible speaks about how this works on many pages but presents its wisdom in an "archaic" manner. Reading and trying to understand ancient scriptures causes many of us to pause, think and explore further, while others may pause, think, and continue what we were doing. To *journey to our true inheritance* requires a faithfulness that can only be found in a mature soul, as it is written in Hebrews 5:14:

"But solid food is for the mature, who by constant use have trained themselves to distinguish good from evil."[3]

The maturity of the soul has nothing to do with the physical age of the individual person. The soul matures to the degree that it is open to finding God's direction through the examples of the Son and by instant guidance of the Spirit, which interacts with us in familiar ways and through supernatural means.

His guidance may come in the form of people, animals, trees, rocks, wind, fire, automobiles, water, equipment, spirits, epiphanies, empty open space – everything! I, actively, listen for thoughts and ideas that "magically" appear while meditating, driving, in the shower, walking in a park or forest, and while listening to people talk in person, on the radio, or on TV, etc. God is Everything and All Things; and inspiration can be "attracted" when our mind is open. Evidence of this phenomena is found throughout the Bible and is also found in Revelation 3:20:

"Behold, I stand at the door, and knock: if any man hear my voice, and open the door, I will come in to him, and will sup with him, and he with me."

I have been on my life's journey long enough to know when He has knocked and I let Him in, and when I ignored Him and suffered poor outcomes. However, the larger problem is when we are unaware that He is knocking at all. This causes us to continue living in darkness and misery and being blind to the fact that we have chosen the path we are on.

In 2012 after an alarming setback in my life, I embarked on a path to rediscover who I am. I maintained just enough hopelessness to know I needed to open the door to God, because I wanted new and different perspectives in my life. I prayed to God often for guidance to help me find my true purpose in this world and continue this practice perpetually every day. The responses I believe I've received could have only come from God, as I would have never, consciously, chosen to do these things myself – and they are good.

I have done some good things with my limited human ability, but I wanted to notice the "unprecedented increase" and abundance in my life and in others that I've heard Joel Osteen, Rick Warren, Bishop TD Jakes, Steve Harvey, and Oprah Winfrey talk about. If God is Everything that is written in the Bible, I made a bold promise to uncover the mystery in my life and share the process.

Much of this journal is written as the Mysteries of God unfold in my life during a *"time for searching,"* (Ecclesiastes 3:6).[4] Since finding enough confidence to be led to the edge of my path by the Holy Spirit to witness the miracles we often miss with daily preoccupations, I've

---

[4] New International Version (NIV), Ecclesiastes 3:6

learned to find joy in small things. If we aren't "smelling the roses" and appreciating the minor things in our lives, we aren't living abundant lives.

I've also documented the conspicuous occurrences that had a three-dimensional presence in my life during my journey since August (2013). These profound observations led me to readings and thoughts that fed my soul with the inspiration I needed to continue on the path to discovering my truth.

A "dimension" can be a noticeably distinctive feature of any kind and so, I applied this description to the recognizable evidence in our *material* reality I needed to understand for my faithful walk with God. God made each of us, uniquely, different according to His Purpose but when our "uniqueness" consistently results in feelings of despair, depression, inadequacy, or any sensation other than wonderful and faithful mostly, we may have chosen a path that is untrue for us. Evaluating the purpose for why we are travelling a road that highlights destructive feelings is appropriate.

Since we perceive life in a kind of "3-D" animation, I wanted to find three meaningful expressions of God to comprehend the impact of experiences that "spoke" to me. The three expressions of God that offered me a balanced understanding for the role God would play in my life were:

1) **my-self, which like you is an individual expression of God in human form and worthy of happiness;**
2) **the Bible as the Word of God is ancient wisdom that reveals its secrets to maturing souls; and**
3) **math, science and music, as elements of a comprehensive language of creation God used to develop the wonders of the universe are offered to us for discovery, worship, and perfecting humility.**

In *Meek Strength*, I reveal an unexpected viewpoint on "meekness" and why I believe it is the most powerful attribute of faithful believers. I affirm that God blesses us most when we surrender to Him, as this is the ultimate way of expressing faithfulness. After establishing a unique business model and the money saved to cover first-year expenses runs out, who should I call? Knowing and understanding that God will provide everything we need to fulfill His Perfect Will in our lives requires a soul maturity that can only be found with *meek strength*.

Pannell Enterprises LLC is the company that has been an outgrowth of the emphasis I placed on meekness. It was not until I asked God for help and left my full-time career with a high salary and benefits, that I discovered what being faithful really is. To receive our true inheritance, we must endure a progression of challenges and breakthroughs that await us. The *path to our inheritance* is not to be recognized as easy or difficult to travel like a long walk with hills, flat lands, rocky paths, and straight roads. It's only a journey if we are trying to get to the end of it. The challenges of our journey are to mature our souls and as such, we should look for opportunities to balance difficult hills with inspiring music or an audiobook, etc.

Furthermore, it is much harder to continue a life that is untrue for us than it is to seek the abundance that God has for us. But fear will talk the majority of us out of taking the journey. I believe God prepared the way before we were born by writing the "program script" with the essential answers, people and opportunities all around us for accomplishment. God will lead us to the *edge of the water line*, if we ask, but we must choose to take a drink.

For readers interested in exploring their tallest dream, this journal offers collective wisdom from Biblical, historical, ancient literary, and scientific sources and my personal journey to business ownership and beyond as a reference – all in one space. Vivid awareness of the information offered here empowered me to establish full-time operations for one company, Pannell Enterprises LLC, which led to the launch of two business units named Food Vending Solutions and Fridge On Wheels Rentals, within three months of my initial business start. The astonishing success of my company's debut offers a true perspective for hungry seekers looking for enough inspiration to take their next step.

I believe and offer observable evidence that a collective faith in spiritual solutions – at this moment – is the ONLY counterweight to all we see going "mysteriously" along a destructive path in our communities and global society. We were created to appreciate life on earth, as we journey to recognize a distinct spiritual/material balance that God intends for us to, individually, achieve. Ancient literature, including the Bible, inform us that we were created in human form to be led by the Spirit, and scientific exploration has confirmed the presence of God in our *material* reality.

If this book touches a place in your mind and heart, please follow the instructions on the last page for how to become an MSA member. My hope is that many people will find this information helpful and encouraging, but there may be some who are not open to the nature of this approach. Consequently, I'm reminded "the lips of wisdom are closed except to the ears of understanding,"[5]

---

[5] *The Kybalion*, by Three Initiates, (1912), http://www.sacred-texts.com/eso/kyb/kyb04.htm

TABLE OF CONTENTS

INTRODUCTION

I recently recalled as a child around age nine attending Sunday school and learning about the Beatitudes, which Jesus Christ offered during the Sermon on the Mount. The first one of eight says: *"Blessed are the poor in spirit: for theirs is the kingdom of heaven"* (Matthew 5:3). It took numerous years of challenging life experiences to approach some understanding of why Jesus chose these circumstances. Many of us don't even think they apply to us and view as issues for society's incapable and oppressed populations.

Since Jesus spoke in parables, we are forced to think our way through why He would say such things. Who are the *poor in spirit*? According to the great evangelist, Billy Graham, they are the humble individuals who understand their own "spiritual emptiness and poverty," so when they come to God pride doesn't get in the way of their blessings.[6] In short, for us to have the Kingdom of Heaven, we must be poor in spirit. This appears simple in theory right?

For some reason, I've always been drawn to the Beatitudes, because even though I wasn't sure how to apply the meanings of the teachings to my life, I knew they were important. My favorite of all Beatitudes is *"Blessed are the meek: for they will inherit the earth,"* (Matthew 5:5). Even though I never liked the term "meek" until recently, I've always viewed the statement as very powerful: the meek will inherit the earth! Said another way, the earth is the inheritance of the meek. Wow! I always associated meekness with weakness, pushover, walkover, and head-down qualities, but that was before Sunday, August 18, 2013.

While developing criteria and an organizational structure for an academy to train entrepreneurs on developing ideas into viable business plans, I experienced an epiphany. Due to the vast challenges

---

[6] Billy Graham, *Answers* (September 1, 2004) http://billygraham.org/answer/what-does-it-mean-to-be-poor-in-spirit-as-jesus-said-we-ought-to-be/

I experienced for two years transforming my ideas into real business prospects, I discovered that all "new" business concepts and their authors are met with instant skepticism on day one. Believing that scarce support and my lack of *material* resources were significant obstacles to realizing my vision, I invited frustration and doubt to the party without invitations.

Unfortunately, it is a normal part of human nature to doubt and even criticize our ideas but most of us become discouraged before we get started. My experiences and the historic accounts of famous business innovators reveal that ideas and the beliefs in them are tested before they become real. Upon realizing this truth I wanted to establish an organized method for encouraging other individuals with a talent and hunger for implementing their unique ideas in a practical and meaningful way. In this manner, I hope to broaden the outlook for advancing the social and economic consciousness in the communities we live in.

The "epiphany" I mentioned earlier is an ancient Greek word described as a sudden "manifestation or appearance" that normally leads to leap in understanding. That Sunday afternoon I was immediately overwhelmed by the word "meek" and it was so compelling that I stopped what I was working on to research the term.

I found that meekness was a description, originally, applied to wild horses that had their stubborn determinations "broken" and were trained to be used as war horses. The term meek is translated from the ancient Greek word "praus," which means power under control.[7] I believe the practice of Biblical scripture is so powerful that when a simple term like meekness becomes functional, it makes a beautiful and potent statement.

Since horses are easily spooked with a mounted rider or not, a horse trained for battle would not be scared at all. In fact, a meek horse would ride with or follow his master straight into the line of fire or into the depths of hell. A meek horse is also gentle enough for children to

---

[7] Theodore J. Nottingham, The Journey of the Anointed One: Breakthrough to Spiritual Encounter (Theosis Books 2013).

ride and interact with. God loves gentle and kind but, He needs us to, fearlessly, pursue His Purpose for our lives like war horses.

I read scriptures relating to the Sermon on the Mount and other relevant teachings I rediscovered on the Internet. For additional clarity, I also contacted Dr. C. Lewis Motley for guidance, who at the time was pastor of Elkhorn Baptist Church in the community where I grew up. About three hours later, I was endowed with enough guidance to understand that meekness is more than humility; more than kindness; and more than gentleness. I understand meekness to be *recognition of the Divine Creator being in control, so we control our own acts of strength through Divine Intelligence of the Holy Spirit, with faith that God will intervene in His time as the All Powerful Force.*

In my journal, I write about the natural human experiences that bred confusion for me because of a "mis-education" in society that contributed to a separation of my-*self* from my *spiritual* nature. Science has recently identified a subtle energy or *material* substance that surrounds us and fills all the spaces that look empty. We can neither see, hear, taste nor smell it, but we feel and perceive it every day. That's the Mind of God! Our ancient ancestors were aware of this eternal substance more than 4,000 years ago and without the enhanced technologies we have now.

The "evolution of humanity" is required at this place and time in our vast universe to prepare us for a world of peace, which is also mentioned as Biblical prophecy. However, as we can see there is still much work to do, and each one of us has a role to play in this performance. As an individual whose doubt made it impossible for me to be comfortable with my relationship with God, I offer my "tested" perspectives here during a season of faithful transformation. I present a compelling mystery or my-story, which seeks to demonstrate that meekness is the only method for achieving our tallest dream in the *material* world.

"The heart of man plans his way, but the Lord establishes his steps," *(Proverbs 16:9 ESV).*[8]

---

[8] English Standard Version (ESV), Proverbs 16:9

Our thoughts are much more important to our *material* and *spiritual* realities than previously believed. A combination of thought and emotion inspires a feeling in our bodies that result in transformations of our personal and social environments. To make advanced changes in society, we must transform our-*selves* first. It's rather easy to read and learn new information, but how do we practically implement these new ideas? The answer is: we can make any change that is necessary in our lives when there is a strong enough incentive. These concerns and how I believe the meek inherit the earth will be explored further, as I attempt to reconcile my journey with what I believe is God's Will for my life.

"And why do you worry about clothes? See how the flowers of the field grow. They do not labor or spin." – Matthew 6:28

PART ONE
You Need to Work Hard And Have Passion

My personal journey after graduating high school led me on a three-year stint in the U.S. Army with tours in Germany, the Persian Gulf and Texas; 11-years of post-high school education; college internships in Virginia state agencies, the federal government, and a senator's office; two and a half years working for a nonprofit veterans organization; a 13-year career in the Federal government; three years as an entrepreneur; and a short career in postal operations and distribution. I considered myself an over-achiever as an adult, and being meek never occurred to me.

I believed that God had molded me to be the best I could be through the unique gifts I observed to be good, and if I worked hard enough, I could achieve anything. What I discovered is that even if we are the best at something, and we work the hardest at something, and we feel we deserve something, and most everyone else feels we deserve something, we still may not get it…ever. The question to ask ourselves is this: "is what we think we deserve the Will of God?"

I thought God must have a great sense of humor because when I told my friends, family, bosses and co-workers that I was leaving my "secure" white collar job to start a frozen food distribution company, the look of confusion was classically stamped on their faces. Known only to a few people was that I had achieved everything I had set out to do in my professional career, and then I concluded there must be more to life.

For the first seven years, I tirelessly chased professional opportunities to have an impactful public service career, and was promoted to a higher pay grade every single year for six years. Many people may have observed me as "successful" because I worked extremely hard with an enduring passion to achieve my professional goals. But I was shaded by dark clouds that contributed to a lack of inner joy, and this was growing immensely day by day.

By definition "passion" means to suffer; remember *The Passion of the Christ*?[9] Jesus was crucified for all Humanity. Socrates, Martin Luther King, Jr., St. Catherine of Alexandria, Joan of Arc, St Agatha, and many other faithful individuals were persecuted and killed because of their extraordinary confrontations over the imbalances in established society.

What are we willing to suffer for? Is it for more pay, to accomplish our goals, to please our boss, to raise money for a campaign, to achieve more education, for honors and awards, or other *material* gains? Well, after we die because of our passion, we are no longer able to enjoy the things we suffered for. We need to be sure we express passion where it means the most for both our *material* and *spiritual* pursuits. Misplaced passion leads to insignificant suffering for limited purposes expressed through the ego of *self*.

In the movie, *Saving Private Ryan*, Captain John H. Miller and a group of soldiers sacrifice their lives to save one Army soldier named Private Ryan. As Captain Miller dies, he whispers the following statement to Private Ryan: "earn this."[10] This final declaration offered an opportunity not for further suffering to honor Captain Miller's and the other soldiers' sacrifices, but to preserve life in a way that encourages Private Ryan and others to live in a self-less manner.

Since Jesus was the Final Sacrifice for all believers, we no longer

---

[9] *The Passion of the Christ* Film
[10] *Saving Private Ryan* Film

17

need to suffer to advance our lives as long as we submit to the Will of God for our True Inheritance. In the Biblical Hebrews 10:11-18, it restates that One Sacrifice made the "Covenant" or God's Promise perfect forever, without further sacrifice for it.

[11]Day after day every priest stands and performs his religious duties; again and again he offers the same sacrifices, which can never take away sins. [12] But when this priest had offered for all time one sacrifice for sins, he sat down at the right hand of God, [13] and since that time he waits for his enemies to be made his footstool. [14] For by one sacrifice he has made perfect forever those who are being made holy. [15] The Holy Spirit also testifies to us about this. First he says: [16] "This is the covenant I will make with them after that time, says the Lord. I will put my laws in their hearts, and I will write them on their minds." [17] Then he adds: "Their sins and lawless acts I will remember no more." [18] And where these have been forgiven, sacrifice for sin is no longer necessary. (Hebrews 10:11-18, NIV)[11]

Submitting to God doesn't mean there won't be bad days or hard times on the journey. It means, precisely, that God has the answer for whatever happens as long as we believe. In this example, we exhibit the *meek strength* needed to observe that passion is inadequate for ourselves, and maximized only by *being led to the edge of our path* by the Holy Spirit.

In 2004 and halfway through the most ambitious seven years of my life, my father's dad, Tanner Pannell, died and returned to the Infinite Source of Life. I had just seen him a few days before he passed and knew he was near death. I felt an immediate and massive sense of emptiness that was not curbed through more accomplishments and promotions that I continuously pursued.

Since I was eight years old, and until I left home at 18 for the Army, I had spent almost every day with him in the country grocery store learning many *spiritual* and earthly truths. I closely watched the lively manner in which he greeted customers, his faithful attitude of

---

[11] New International Version (NIV), Hebrews 10:11-18

joy that never appeared troubled, and the humility he exhibited every night while on his knees praying before getting into bed.

He practiced Godliness in a manner, daily, which consistently demonstrated a controlled strength – a meek power. He was so unique and had made such an imprint on my life that I made a silent promise to find a way to continue his legacy. In hindsight, I didn't realize that his "legacy" was not simply that of a renown self-made and wealthy entrepreneur with less than a third grade formal education.

Tanner Pannell's legacy is summarized and best understood by viewing it through a lens that can perceive *meek strength*. However, my own personal issues were layered in such a way that I would not, instantly, find meekness to be easy nor comforting given my daily interactions in the "real" world.

Following my grandfather's death I enrolled in a graduate business program at a Jesuit university on a part-time basis to pursue an MBA, while continuing to work full-time. By this time I was married and my wife and I were raising our first son. I began to realize that my ultimate plan to attend law school was rapidly slipping away as I awaited the "perfect" time to enroll.

My primary objective after completing a bachelor's degree in 1997 was to enroll in law school and by this time I had postponed applying twice. Trivial life circumstances impeded me from recognizing that if my "dream" was to graduate law school, I needed to define those objectives instead of delaying the prospect. I had already taken the Law School Admission Test (LSAT) twice and wasn't confident that I would be accepted to even an average ranked law school in the late 90's, since admittance was extremely competitive.

The overachiever outlook I adopted had convinced me that I needed more professional experience, extra graduate degrees, high-profile references, a higher LSAT score, LSAT preparation courses to get a higher LSAT score, and law school visits, etc. Coincidentally, I left business school after three years of part-time study and decided not to complete the MBA program, or go to law school feeling completely burned out. Did my law school vision drift away, simply, because I exhausted myself, or was my journey redirected in another direction under a different *anointing*? Hmmm…let's explore.

According to Rev. Henry Walker, "anointing is the hammer that nails favor on the circumstances."[12] I understand this to mean that all believers receive the Favor we don't deserve through Grace, a *gift* granted by the death and resurrection of Jesus Christ. When God anoints an individual to carry out a specific objective in the *material* world, Favor will change real circumstances; but only if we are "under control" of the Spirit.

According to Kenneth Copeland, "anointing is God's presence by the Holy Spirit."[13] This brings me right back to the subject of meekness, which is controlled power by the Holy Spirit. I've observed that if our personal goals are not aligned with our anointing, during our journey toward self-actualization, we'll be tired, full of anxiety, confused, and unhappy to say the least.

Based on Psalm 139:13-16 and Jeremiah 1:5, I have a need to believe that God knew me as spirit before I was born and so, I was born into the world to accomplish His Purpose. This purpose is my own personal anointing. We spend our entire lives searching for ideas and meaning, and the answers are all round us. Once born into this life, we somehow forget our true anointing and aimlessly look to TV, friends, and family to affirm our personal journey as adults.

I'm convinced without conclusive evidence that many of us shrink from following our anointed *path* from the start, because for some of us the likelihood of achievement is not self-evident. So without firm affirmation for our initial feelings about a given idea or plan from our family and friends, we try out the familiar *path* that leads to the similar destinations of relatives and friends.

We carefully avoid the detours offering inspired learning because they get in the way of our desired timetable. We often misapply the label of "focus" to refuse all opportunities that may delay but not derail our goals. If the goals we establish are true for us, time never creates a dilemma

---

[12] Rev. Henry Walker website, *God's Favor and the Anointing!* http://henrywalker.org/message143.htm

[13] Kenneth Copeland, *Understanding the Anointing* http://www.kcm.org/real-help/article/understanding-anointing

for achievement. This has been a difficult lesson for me to accept.

As believers why do we place so much emphasis on the *material* world when we "faithfully" acknowledge that we are *material* flesh with a *spiritual* essence? We are spirit manifested in the flesh to do God's Will, and if we apply His Divine Laws on the road to relearning who we are, we get to stop and smell the roses along the way. I don't remember who said it first but "when you walk in your anointing, it follows you wherever you go." You are unable to escape it!

Unfortunately, or maybe fortunately for us, working hard and being passionate aren't enough to accomplish the goal for which we were anointed. They are only part of the equation. There are some, who are born into the world and right away are mathematical geniuses and musical prodigies.

One perspective might express that their souls were mature enough to walk right down their anointed *path* without delay or impediment. For most of us, however, our souls must continue to mature through our daily interactions in the *material* world and by reaching out to Divine Intelligence of the Spirit for assistance.

Without complete self-absorption we must consciously think about who we are, observe our daily interactions, and ponder why God permitted our existence among our friends and families at this time in His-story (history). There is a purpose. Aristotle once stated that "contemplation is the highest form of action."[14]

It took me several years of contemplating that statement to understand that whatever you are consistently thinking about is who you really are. Our thoughts dictate our actions, how we feel, and create the place in the world we live in. With that said, there is no chance for us to achieve our real goals and follow our true purpose without a consistent belief and faith in the "inner idea" that energizes us every time we think about or are exposed to it.

This inner idea will manifest as an inner voice that becomes loud chatter over a lifetime when we don't listen to it. I believe this inner

---

[14] Aristotle: Contemplative Life is Divine and Happiest: https://satyagraha.wordpress.com/2018/10/13/aristotle-contemplative-life/

voice is the anointing of the Spirit that supernaturally communes with us. At times, it coerces us to listen through circumstances we perceive as God punishing us or withdrawing Favor from us.

I do not believe that God imposes extreme punishments on His Flesh, but He does allow situations to affect our lives. Please consider the discussion between God and Satan in the oldest book of the bible, Job. The enemy, Satan, makes a solemn request to God to harm Job, in order to prove that human faith in God is no match for *material* suffering. Since the Supreme Alpha and the Omega knows the beginning and ending of every situation, he approves Satan's request to attack Job, *materially*, to teach our enemy, Job, and Humanity a fruitful lesson.

"⁶One day the angels came to present themselves before the LORD, and Satan also came with them. ⁷The LORD said to Satan, "Where have you come from?" Satan answered the LORD, "From roaming throughout the earth, going back and forth on it." ⁸Then the LORD said to Satan, "Have you considered my servant Job? There is no one on earth like him; he is blameless and upright, a man who fears God and shuns evil." ⁹ "Does Job fear God for nothing?" Satan replied. ¹⁰ "Have you not put a hedge around him and his household and everything he has? You have blessed the work of his hands, so that his flocks and herds are spread throughout the land. ¹¹But now stretch out your hand and strike everything he has, and he will surely curse you to your face." ¹²The LORD said to Satan, "Very well, then, everything he has is in your power, but on the man himself do not lay a finger." Then Satan went out from the presence of the LORD." (Job 1:6-12, NIV)[15]

Remember when crises in our lives demand our complete attention, He is aware and has also, approved this intervention. My Lord...but why would You allow the most dreadful and awful acts of violence to happen to Your most faithful and weakest citizens? He attempts to advise us in Isaiah 55:8: *"For my thoughts are not your*

---

[15] New International Version (NIV), Job 1:6-12

thoughts, neither are your ways my ways, declares the LORD." And after wandering and journeying for my entire life up till now, I accept this simple rationale. It is impossible for us to, entirely, understand our Powerful Creator, but He has offered us everything in our surroundings to provide a glimpse into His Thinking.

When an experienced cook decides to bake a cake, all of the ingredients are placed on the counter for easy access. With a dab of this and a splash of that, a mixture is contrived that only the cook (creator) has a specific knowledge of. The cook also knows how long to bake, how long to cool before icing, and how it is supposed to taste. Imagine the creator of this cake knowing what other complements he wants to serve with cake, and maybe, what variety of drinks will chase each tasty ration. However, the cake does not understand its place in the world, but if it did it would, likely, choose to free itself from being enjoyed by us – even though, that is its true purpose.

There are consequences for not seeking and finding our Divine Purpose, since that is why we are here in the first place. I've heard it my entire life and now I believe it's true in accordance with Matthew 7:7, which says:

"Ask and it will be given to you; seek and you will find; knock and the door will be opened to you." [16]

This Biblical scripture and many others reflect Spiritual-Universal Laws that promise if you look for Divine Truth and Purpose you will find it. Furthermore, when you identify your tallest dream and believe that God wants you to take the journey, meaningful accomplishment is to be expected.

On this journey, our fear companion is never late and shows up early to cloud our decisions because the finish line is, partially, concealed. But with faithfulness comes the anticipation of good things that inspire us to keep progressing. Open the door to fear but give him the back seat! We sit in the driver's seat and allow Divine Intelligence

---

[16] New International Version (NIV), Matthew 7:7

of the Spirit to hold the directions for guidance along the way.

Fear will attempt to be a backseat driver by yelling, "turn left; turn right; hurry up; yellow light means green; and you can drive nine miles per hour over the speed limit on the sign, because the police set the radar gun at 10 miles per hour over the speed limit!" Our response is: "I hear you fear, but shut up! I stand on the solid rock of Jesus Christ! What do you have to say about this Holy Spirit?"

Passion and hard work will not rule the day on the journey toward our true inheritance, as it is written *"for my yoke is easy and my burden is light,"* (Matthew 11:30).17 It is promised that if we place our *material* burdens on the All Powerful Creative Force, the Source of Divine Light and Love, and open our "inner ear" to Divine Intelligence of the Spirit everything we need will be offered along the way.

The lack of *material* resources such as education, money, experience, and references won't matter because our true *path* was established before we were born. If I had not observed these supernatural phenomena in "real time" I would have no testimony to share. God's Promise is True!

God prepares us for abundance
8"Praise our God, all peoples, let the sound of his praise be heard; 9he has preserved our lives and kept our feet from slipping. 10 For you, God, tested us; you refined us like silver. 11You brought us into prison and laid burdens on our backs. 12 You let people ride over our heads; we went through fire and water, but you brought us to a place of abundance." (Psalm 66:5-7, NIV)18

God's Will is our True Purpose
1"Can you pull in Leviathan with a fishhook or tie down its tongue with a rope? 2 Can you put a cord through its nose or pierce its jaw with a hook? 3 Will it keep begging you for mercy? Will it speak to you with gentle words? 4 Will it make an agreement with you for you to take it as your slave

---

17 New International Version (NIV), Matthew 11:30
18 New International Version (NIV), Psalm 66:5-7

24

for life? 5 Can you make a pet of it like a bird or put it on a leash for the young women in your house? 6 Will traders barter for it? Will they divide it up among the merchants? 7 Can you fill its hide with harpoons or its head with fishing spears? 8 If you lay a hand on it, you will remember the struggle and never do it again! 9 Any hope of subduing it is false; the mere sight of it is overpowering. 10 No one is fierce enough to rouse it. Who then is able to stand against me? 11 Who has a claim against me that I must pay? Everything under heaven belongs to me." (Job 41:1-11, NIV)19

1 Then Job replied to the Lord: 2"I know that you can do all things; no purpose of yours can be thwarted. 3 You asked, 'Who is this that obscures my plans without knowledge?' Surely I spoke of things I did not understand, things too wonderful for me to know. (Job 42:1-3, NIV)20

The Infinite Source of Divine Life and Light is Truth

"1 In the beginning was the Word, and the Word was with God, and the Word was God. 2 He was with God in the beginning. 3 Through him all things were made; without him nothing was made that has been made. 4 In him was life, and that life was the light of all mankind. 5 The light shines in the darkness, and the darkness has not overcome it." (John 1:5, NIV)21

The Holy Spirit inspires our works of creation

25 All this I have spoken while still with you. 26 But the Advocate, the Holy Spirit, whom the Father will send in my name, will teach you all things and will remind you of everything I have said to you. 27 Peace I leave with you; my peace I give you. I do not give to you as the world gives. Do not let your hearts be troubled and do not be afraid." (John 14:26, NIV)22

"1 A shoot will come up from the stump of Jesse; from his roots a Branch will bear fruit. 2 The Spirit of the Lord will rest on him—the Spirit of wisdom

---

19 New International Version (NIV), Job 41:1-11
20 New International Version (NIV), Job 42:1-3
21 New International Version (NIV), John 1:5
22 New International Version (NIV), John 14:26

and of understanding, the Spirit of counsel and of might, the Spirit of the knowledge and fear of the Lord— ³ and he will delight in the fear of the Lord." (Isaiah 11:1-3, NIV)[23]

After my grandfather's death in 2004, I was really in the "dumps," and considered every alternative available to resolve my problems – except turning to God. God is the only Option and He's free, but many of us don't realize this until we reach a mature age; or we never learn in our lifetime. Awareness of the Fullness of God's presence in our lives causes us to make the necessary changes that will lead us only to the *edge of the beginning of our journey*. This is the meaning of "free will" and our full cooperation is required.

As my professional career continued a steady upward climb, my personal happiness and satisfaction declined at the same pace. That was the sign! I could literally feel the walls of discontent closing in on me and at times I couldn't breathe. No matter how well we believe we're doing, or how other people think we're doing, if we aren't feeling beautiful, frequently, we need God's assistance to guide us to the *edge of the beginning of our journey*. We need nothing more than a continuous adverse feeling to know a change needs to be made. Although my stubborn rationalism fed me with fictional narratives for four more years until I, freely, committed to stepping up.

In 2008, I started the quest to build on my spiritual knowledge and rediscovered that I knew many of the Biblical quotes and religious teachings I had orally recited when I was in elementary school; but I was unable to apply them to my personal life. Simply speaking, there was a huge gap between my knowledge of scripture and my ability to work spiritual magic in my life.

As explained, previously, I maintained just enough hopelessness for God to lead me to the *edge of the beginning of my journey*. I was often recognized as a bold personality, since I found pleasure in being the first to do anything with a measure of value. While full of this newfound *spiritual* knowledge and awareness, I needed to download it

---

[23] New International Version (NIV), Isaiah 11:1-3

to others, who could use it through a mass distribution method.

Since writing in my profession was required, I began "masking" spiritual concepts as occupational best practices, and they were, favorably, reviewed and comprehended that way. I was, definitely, on to something, so I continued doing it over the next five years without reluctance or fear that my writings would be misinterpreted. This was a huge victory in self-confidence for me.

Additionally, I found the motivation to start writing business plans as ideas came to me under this anointing, and I ended with five solid business proposals. I prayed often and awaited guidance in the form of specific *material* manifestations, I believed came from Divine Intelligence. With an intense feeling of peace and confidence about being a full-time entrepreneur, I took a leap of faith with the fifth business plan, and not the first one and resigned my job, effectively, April 5, 2013.

Bottom line: on the path to our inheritance we ease our passionate suffering by observing that challenges are a natural part of the journey, and God has already paved the way.

"Rather than putting your thoughts on what is, or what you've habitually thought for a lifetime, you shift to looking up and seeing, and firmly believing in what you see. When you begin to think in this manner, the Universe conspires to work with you, and sends you precisely what you're thinking and believing." – Dr. Wayne W. Dyer

PART TWO
Universal Spiritual Laws of the Cosmos

Many of the Mysteries of God can be found in the synergies of the Universal Laws of the cosmos. In 2008 during a very tumultuous period in my life, I began a search for God and the Spirit because I needed to find a more sustainable path toward a personal vision I was nowhere near attaining. "If Matthew 7:7 is Truth," I felt comfortably sure I would be led on a unique and interesting journey. I immersed myself in Biblical scriptures, ancient literature, metaphysics, science and self-help books.

I believe God is the Infinite Source of all Creation from the beginning to eternity and we are an extension of His Divine Spirit in human flesh to experience the full potential of His Love and Power. It follows logically that we grow stronger in our understanding of the *material* world and our *spiritual* reality by observing how our natural environment intersects with spiritual and universal truths. As I continued to seek my truth, I prayed to God for guidance and meditated to hear the responses in order to feel the absolute peace I've read comes along with realizing Truth in the presence of the Spirit.

I discovered readings on the Principles of the Universe that explain the true nature of interaction between energy and matter. These Principles illustrate how Universal Law drives effective creation in our *material* existence on earth under Divine Providence, and in accordance with the anointing on our lives. However, these forces do not judge the intent of our request and so, often we create a miserable life of depression and isolation associated with our conscious and subconscious thoughts, and emotions. Science has already informed us that all matter is a dense form of energy, which means that our bodies are vibrating energy particles along with our thoughts, emotions, and words.

Our closest source of Life and Light provided by the Love of God is the sun. I knew the sun revolved around something in our universe but I never previously learned about the 26,000 year orbit of our sun in this galaxy; this "revolution was not televised." I bring this up because the sun's revolution around the galaxy impacts conditions here on earth that influence the united potential of humanity.

I strongly believe our lack of awareness of these conditions adversely limits our ability to identify and follow a true *path* to our inheritance. All knowledge and awareness works together for the good of those who love God.[24] If this was not so, this specific knowledge and the ability to access it could not exist.

Newton's Law of Universal Gravitation states that "every point mass in the universe attracts every other point mass with a force that is directly proportional to the product of their masses and inversely proportional to the square of the distance between them."[25] Basically in the "fabric" of the *material* world on earth, whatever goes up must come down. It does not matter whether we agree, acknowledge, understand or even like gravity. This force directs matter to act in an observably predictable manner.

There are many natural laws that intersect with the philosophic principles of Hermetic Philosophy. Hermetic Philosophy originated from societies older than Egypt. The writings are similar to those in

---

[24] Bible Romans 8:28

[25] Wikipedia, Newton's Law of Universal Gravitation http://en.wikipedia.org/wiki/Newton's_law_of_universal_gravitation

our Bible, but have been isolated from Biblical teachings and are more associated with the European Renaissance and scientific theology or alchemy. I mention the seven Hermetic Principles here as a reference for further discovery: Principle of Mentalism, Principle of Cause and Effect, Principle of Vibration, Principle of Rhythm, Principle of Correspondence, Principle of Gender, and Principle of Polarity.[26]

All of humanity and the earth originated from cosmic *material* as the result of an exploding sun (supernova) and we know this because science has taught us all the elements heavier than hydrogen originated inside stars. According to the American Physical Society, 93% of the mass in our body is stardust.[27] Based on these findings, we can conclude that we are not separate entities from each other here on earth or throughout the universe – we are one big cosmic family!

Many scientists today have adopted the origin of our universe based on the predictions of Albert Einstein's Theory of General Relativity. This theory supports that everything in the universe was compressed to the size of a green pea.[28] After the "Big Bang," as some physicists have referred to it, the universe expanded with intense heat and speed. Although it's difficult to imagine that Humanity is One with everything in the universe since we appear to be separate entities, the energy that once united us still exists in the "empty spaces" between us, and is measurable.[29]

Specific research on light energy particles in Geneva, Switzerland revealed that when one light particle (photon) is split into two particles and both are separated by 7 miles, the photons still act like they are connected.[30] Experiments like these remind us that from our single-

---

[26] *The Kybalion*, by Three Initiates, (1912), http://www.sacred-texts.com/eso/kyb/kyb04.htm

[27] American Physical Society, How much of the human body is made up of stardust? http://www.physicscentral.com/explore/poster-stardust.cfm

[28] Nola Taylor Redd, SPACE.com (September 18, 2012) http://www.space.com/17661-theory-general-relativity.html

[29] Nassim Haramein - Sacred Geometry and Unified Fields (April 8, 2012) http://www.youtube.com/watch?v=4zc0ICPoqlM

[30] Malcolm W. Browne, *The New York Times*, Far Apart, 2 Particles Respond Faster Than Light (July 22, 1997) http://www.nytimes.com/1997/07/22/science/far-apart-2-particles-respond-faster-than-light.html?pagewanted=all&src=pm

point beginning, everything in the universe is still connected even though we now exist as individual expressions of God.

Even more profound, a very controversial physicist named, Nassim Haramein, developed a "Unified Field Theory" study, which seeks to demonstrate that the interconnectedness of the whole universe implies geometry, which is the origin of mathematics.[31] "That which is above is from that which is below, and that which is below is from that which is above, working the miracles of one."[32]

Further, we can be considered individual universes with equivalent infinite resources within us, as they exist in the universe. Of course this means we are able to create and manifest God's Potential in our *material* reality. God prepared us all to resolve certain mysteries that we only uncover on the *journey toward our inheritance*. Each of us has an individual truth to discover and share with the world for God's Purpose. Galileo Galilei is reported to have said that God wrote the language of the universe in mathematics and Haramein offers the mathematical premise, which underscores that we all share the same One Consciousness.[33] There is Biblical text that offers evidence for the Law of Unity stated in Genesis 11:5-6:

"But the LORD came down to see the city and the tower which the sons of men had built. And the LORD said, Indeed the people are one and they all have one language, and this is what they begin to do; now nothing that they propose to do will be withheld from them."[34]

It is written that God Almighty witnesses that when humanity tears down the fabricated constructs that divide us in our common pursuits such as race, culture, language, politics, red states and blue states, socioeconomic status, religion, homophobia, Japanophobia,

---

[31] Unified Field Theory – Nassim Haramein: https://www.youtube.com/playlist?list=PLF4A375E5CC1E7B4A

[32] The Emerald Tablet of Hermes, Holmyard 1923: https://www.sacred-texts.com/alc/emerald.htm

[33] Goodreads, Galileo Galilei Quote https://www.goodreads.com/quotes/467246-mathematics-is-the-language-with-which-god-has-written-the

[34] New King James Version (NKJV), Genesis 11:5-6

Judeophobia, xenophobia, etc. – man is able to accomplish anything.

God is Everything and All Things! He uses everyone and everything in the cosmos to accomplish His Purpose. We are to trust God and lean not on our own understanding....as He will work things out in our favor. Additionally we are to judge not because there will come a time for each of us to be judged since all of our imperfections and wrong doings are already recorded in the One Soul of human experience.

As it is written in the Bible, the Book of Life exists with all of the names of people who believe in their salvation and true purpose and so, who has legitimate time to devote to scrutinizing the lives of others?[35] I've realized on my current *path* that I need every ounce of consciousness aligned with faithfulness, patience, forgiveness, love, and gratitude. If we spend most of the time paying attention to the roadmap on our journey, we will be looking for opportunities to demonstrate Divine Love because we will, certainly, need it ourselves at some point. In essence this is also, *meek strength.*

The Law of Attraction within the context of God's Will, and as illustrated in a book entitled *The Secret* should be understood to some degree if you want to purposefully create the incredible life God intended just for us in the *material* world.[36] As mentioned before, we are "energy beings" that are constantly emitting creative energies based on our thoughts, emotions, and feelings. When we feel extremely good we emit energy waves on a frequency that is expressed as high pitch sound-sensation.[37]

This energy sensation broadcasts to all other universal feel good entities on that frequency that we feel good. If we are able to maintain that feeling whether we are aware or not, we "attract" experiences to us that correspond with that good feeling. Quantum physics teaches us that all matter vibrates at the subatomic particle level at a certain speed

---

[35] English Standard Version (ESV), Revelation 20:12

[36] Rhonda Byrne, *The Secret* (New York: Atria Books/Beyond Words, 2006)

[37] Cymatics: Sacred Geometry Formed by Sound http://www.youtube.com/watch?v=vFRtjZ3NrqM

even though we see things that appear to be solid.[38] So it is realistic for a person to give off and feel a vibe, which happens to be sound waves vibrating on a frequency we can feel.

In our *material* reality, we create the world we live in 24-hours a day by attracting into our lives what we consistently think and "feel" about.[39] During the most ambitious period of my life, I had a keen awareness of the college scholarships, summer internships, and jobs that I intended to apply for and would ultimately receive. Before I became, fully, aware of the Law of Attraction, I believed that passion, studying, hard work, belief in myself and prayer was enough to pursue anything, successfully.

If that approach was enough to reach our tallest dream, I believe more people would be living the life of their dreams. The creation of a dream life involves a clear vision of what that looks like. Instead of creating a clear vision for our dreams, we often disregard our dreams as fantasy to focus on working hard to pay bills, supporting our family, receiving recognition, getting promoted, becoming famous, or obtaining riches; and maybe even all of those things.

At one time, I even believed the more money I earned, the more money I would have in my pocket. That is a myth. It's the more money I save and invest using the power of compound interest – the more money I will have in my pocket. The path can become long, difficult and hopeless when we begin a mythical journey.

A clear vision for our life, contemplation on the intent of our vision, continuous prayer, faithful thoughts with feelings of joy and gratitude, and discussions with someone we trust to support this dream vision will stimulate the "magnetic" creative energies necessary to benefit from the Law of Attraction. Again, thoughts are energy particles that will manifest an idea in physical form as something favorable or unpleasant at some time, based on the primary themes of our conscious and subconscious thoughts and emotions.[40]

---

[38] John Assaraf, Achieve Even More http://johnassaraf.com/law-of-attractionwhy-you-should-be-aware-of-quantum-physics-2

[39] Rhonda Byrne, *The Secret* (New York: Atria Books/Beyond Words, 2006)

[40] Rhonda Byrne, *The Secret* (New York: Atria Books/Beyond Words, 2006)

According to the Discovering Psychology & Study Guide, emotions involve a complex psychological state with three distinct components: a subjective experience, a physiological response, and a response expressed as a behavior.[41] The content of our thoughts and emotions influence the feelings we act on, and if we are not careful about the ideas we consistently think about, our life creations begin to work against us.

These thought energies attract the people we interact with on a daily basis, which are those people who are vibrating on the same frequency. So "birds of a feather do flock together." My observations and experiences have taught me there is no distance or obstacle large enough to keep "like-thought" generators from attracting each other. It doesn't matter whether this attraction happens for business, dating, or conspiracy purposes.

Since our lives are the Providence of God, He allows us to attract the necessary people and "ingredients" to our lives based on the issues we think about most. We should monitor and evaluate our most common thoughts and ideas to ensure they are consistent with intended outcomes. The Biblical text that offers evidence for this "magical" phenomena is:

"Again I say to you, that if two of you agree on earth about anything that they may ask, it shall be done for them by My Father who is in heaven. For where two or three have gathered together in My name, I am there in their midst." (Matthew 18:19-20, ESV)[42]

Many scientists have accepted that our human existence is much more than *material*. There is firm evidence all over the world that supports the perspective that our ancient ancestors knew this at least 3,000 years ago! The inscriptions they left for us validate that we were born to worship the Divine Creator, as the original interpretations of

---

[41] Don H. Hockenbury, Sandra E. Hockenbury, 4th Edition, Discovering Psychology & Study Guide (2007).
[42] English Standard Version (ESV), Matthew 18:19-20

our universe have been determined by many scholars to be exact.[43] The Divine Laws of the cosmos have been a protected secret in the modern age, while imbedded in Biblical text for those who are led by God and the Spirit to live their lives on purpose.

We are able to use inspirational forces the Creator has endowed the universe with to influence our *material* world. These forces surround us as powerful, subtle vibrations from us and among us. I discovered when I'm generating destructive thoughts induced by anger, frustration, anxiety, sadness or depression, I am in fact creating something in my environment resonating on the "destroy matter" frequency – a low pitch sensation. This frequency is sometimes associated with the onset of illness, and may have progressed my body's development of type 1 insulin dependent diabetes in 2000. The whole time we believe things are just happening by chance, and we may be producing these "ill" effects ourselves.

Believe it or not, we have to find ways to trick our-*selves* into thinking adequate thoughts as needed, in a way that makes sense for us. There was an episode in *Seinfeld,* one of my favorite "sitcoms," where George, the best friend of the main character, agrees to make the opposite choice for all future decisions under any situation. For example, if his normal response would have been no, the opposite response now of course, would be yes.

George believes this new philosophy will change his life by offering the reverse effect of his present condition. In his mind, he is already on the bottom step of life and there is no place to go but up. However funny that episode is intended to be, the theme was very profound to me. This episode was the inspiration for me to make life-changing modifications for daily thoughts, while dealing with adverse conditions near the *edge of the beginning of my journey.* Just think the opposite! When we are open to it, God makes all things work for us – even comedies like *Seinfeld.*

I, actively, believe that optimism and affirmative dialogue is

---

[43] Drunvalo Melchizedek, (1999). *The Ancient Secret of the Flower of Life Volume 1.* Light Technology Publishing.

so important that I spend most of my personal time evaluating both my conscious and subconscious thoughts – all the time. It's when we are, frequently, unfocused and allow negativity to crack the door and tiptoe inside that we accept our weakest moments. We actually unlock the door to those emotions and, subconsciously, invite them in. Also consider that we become the product of what we think about, mostly, and our world is created and shaped out of that reflection.

My goal is to "access" the same frequency of all other souls practicing or searching for *meek strength* opportunities so we learn from each other and compel our *material* world toward a more magnificent and enlightened existence. We become powerful spirits in our *material* incarnation when we submit to God's Purpose for our lives and swim in the ocean of cosmic music that creates and supports the *journey to our inheritance.*

I no longer obsess about the needs on my journey, since I want to attract peaceful experiences while on the "yellow brick" *path.* On this journey the yellow brick *path* represents the golden path to our inheritance, but with a twist.[44] The "Wonderful Wizard" travels with us and grants our entry to all essential gateways as long as we exhibit patience and thankfulness. I believe the display of patience and gratitude under all circumstances invokes the *meek strength* we need to overcome every obstacle.

Fear will continue to open the door and peek inside to offer unwanted input on our decisions. He's like an annoying neighbor that interrupts us at the worst possible moment to borrow something you don't have, and then just hangs around when you tell him you don't have what he wants. We may even anticipate frustration and doubt creeping up behind fear, but this is a natural part of our *material* human nature. We must acknowledge and listen to our emotions and feelings, as we learn something about ourselves and our journey when we listen.

Bottom line: our thoughts, emotions, and feelings are aspects of a cosmic language that vibrate on quantum frequencies throughout our universe to produce the ideas in physical form we are faithful to.

---

[44] The Wizard of Oz (1939)

"Happiness for a reason is just another form of misery
because the reason can be taken away from us at any time."
– Deepak Chopra

PART THREE
Happiness is an Illusion

I had a humorous childhood buddy, who could turn the simplest of observations into the funniest comments. Although he remarked, seriously, we laughed, hysterically, and agreed that the statement was likely true. One of the strangest comments I ever heard from him one day was that he didn't enjoy being happy because his experiences had taught him his entire life that something bad would, immediately, happen and ruin everything. However gloomy that statement seemed to me at the time, I also felt it was true that happiness is temporary.

The happiness that is defined for us in our popular culture through music, videos, movies, magazines, and photos and on the Internet is short-lived at best. I think many of us believe we need something or someone else to make us happy. That is a myth. The path can become long, difficult and hopeless when we begin a mythical journey. I used to think happiness was separate and apart from me and that specific moments, occasions, and things were a part of my environment to generate happiness. That's what these things are for right? It took me a while to even consider that sustainable happiness is found on the inside and radiates out like rays of sunshine.

According to Wikipedia, "happiness is a mental or emotional state of well-being characterized by positive or pleasant emotions ranging from contentment to intense joy."[45] The key portion of the definition for me is "mental or emotional state of well-being." To get to a steady mental or emotional state of well-being requires a continuous practice of optimistic thinking. Even though joy is considered a synonym for happiness, I perceive joy to be a more significant level of achievement. Biblical scriptures endowed with many Spiritual-Universal Laws frequently refer to joy more so than happiness. I make a distinction between happiness and joy, only because the scriptures proclaim that joy comes from God as in Romans 15:13:

"May the God of hope fill you with all joy and peace in believing, so that by the power of the Holy Spirit you may abound in hope." [46]

During our never-ending search for happiness, we overlook that joy is a "fruit" or noticeable outcome achieved from obtaining the free gifts from God offered through the Spirit. The Spirit eternally seeks us out to present us with this endowment – but only when we are open to receiving it.[47] Traditionally these seven gifts have been presented as wisdom, understanding, counsel, knowledge, strength, piety (reverence), and fear of the Lord (awe). Joy is divine and to me has a supernatural origin since it is available to us during good and bad times (Isaiah 11:1-3).

By virtue of being human in our *material* world, I believe we balance a naturally occurring state of dualism. This dual nature keeps our emotions in constant flux swinging like a *pendulum* between happy and sad, good thoughts and bad thoughts, angry and calm, excited and disinterested, and many more normal feelings. Dualism does not mean, however, that both extremes are separate and apart from each other. Just the opposite – both extremes are reverse sides of the same coin; heads and tales! This exemplifies the Universal Principle of Polarity.[48]

---

[45] Wikipedia, Happiness http://en.wikipedia.org/wiki/Happiness

[46] English Standard Version (ESV), Romans 15:13

[47] New King James Version (NKJV), Galatians 5:22-23

[48] *The Kybalion*, by Three Initiates, (1912), http://www.sacred-texts.com/eso/kyb/kyb04.htm

My mother simplified this for me when I was in my early teens. She told me that when we are experiencing the storms and turbulence of life, we are to buckle down, hold on, and ride it out because on the other side of this turmoil is a blessing! I have applied this wisdom to balance the emotional swings in my life ever since, while knowing that when daylight comes, night fall is imminent; on a rainy day, sunshine is on its way; and when sadness looms, something good will soon emerge.

I look forward to the vibrant radiance of a rainbow after a life-storm, as I'm confident there is a metaphorical or real pot of gold nearby. God wants us to calmly endure by resting in the awareness of His Power, and it is written in scripture that states... *"Be still, and know that I am God,"*.[49] We don't need to suffer alone as God wants to be a safe haven for comfort and resolve. Our life experiences are His as well.

Einstein enlightened us with his celebrated physics equation $E=mc^2$, which means the mass of an object is equal to its energy content; matter and energy are equal.[50] Additionally, all matter is equal to itself and all energy is equal to itself; the only difference is *form*.[51] We are created with the ability to balance our pain and pleasure sensations, good and bad thoughts, and happy and sad mood swings, as these energies are layers of the same energy field.

This concept of opposites as they are represented in dualism is also symbolized by the Chinese yin and yang forces that manifest as hot and cold, life and death, and good and evil, etc. Even though these opposing forces convey two extremes, the two are mutually dependent on each other in a recurring cycle of cooperation, in order for us to understand the complexities of both ideas.

For example, to fully appreciate breathing fresh air, try holding your breath underwater in a swimming pool for a minute and the next gulp of air becomes the best one ever! We don't even notice that we

---

[49] New International Version (NIV), Psalms 46:1-10

[50] Peter Tyson, The Legacy of E = mc² http://www.pbs.org/wgbh/nova/physics/legacy-of-e-equals-mc2.html

[51] Ibid.

are breathing from moment to moment but when air is taken from us, we are immediately thankful to have it back. In addition, how can you truly appreciate water if you've never been thirsty? The same applies to experiencing less than good times in our lives. The *pendulum of equilibrium* swings back and forth to allow us to acknowledge – out loud (praise) and appreciate how truly good the good times really are.

The law of diminishing returns, which normally applies in economics, can also be applied to happiness. The law says that as a factory adds new employees to manufacture a certain product, at some point each additional employee that comes aboard will produce less than the previous employee.[52] As this applies to happiness, once we've achieved it in any area of life, more gains in that specific area contribute less and less to our happiness.

When I was about five years old, I asked my mom for a Spiderman action figure for Christmas. Unfortunately, that year Spiderman was very popular and all the stores had sold out. On Christmas morning I opened up gifts with Superman and Batman, but not the superhero I really wanted. I remember being happy and having plenty of stuff that Christmas but not having Spiderman was, obviously, memorable to me.

My mother made sure I eventually got the Spiderman I always wanted on another occasion and I played with it every day with animated excitement until one day I just stopped playing with it. I had used Spiderman to defeat all the enemy toys and when that got boring, he fought Batman and Superman. He had been tied to the top of the stairs and swung to the bottom many times. Spiderman had fought in the bathtub and defeated villains wet and finished the battles out of the tub while drying off. After a while, the more I played with the Spiderman toy, the longer breaks I took from playing with it. Happiness with this toy had run its course, and I couldn't squeeze any more from it!

This scenario represents the law of diminishing returns as it

---

[52] Investopedia, Law of Diminishing Marginal Returns http://www.investopedia. com/terms/l/lawofdiminishingmarginalreturn.asp

applies to our interactions in the *material* world. However, this law does not govern our interactions with the Spirit, which constantly offers joy to us at every given moment when we stop overlooking the small miracles in our lives.

These miracles greet us when we leave home late and arrive to work on time; when there is no money in the bank and a check shows up unexpectedly; and for example, when "marital relations" create the perception of a new beginning scare, and a test reassures there is still enough time to plan. Being in the present to be, intentionally, aware of a miracle offers joy without looking for it. There is still more about the gifts and being present to acknowledge and receive I'm trying to explore and understand further.

I remember in elementary school when our home classroom teacher would conduct roll-call by calling out our last names first and our response to this would be "present." Well, if your last name began with a letter that was further along in the alphabet like mine, your opportunity for distractions was increased by the number of seconds it took the teacher to call on you. If you were present in the moment the response to your name being called would have been "present" or "here," but if you were not, your response may have been "huh?"

Being present in the moment means that you are fully aware of distractions so you are not distracted and at the same time, you are aware of favorable aspects in your surroundings. In the previous example, being alert to say "present" would be a good start and other examples of being in the moment would include a vibrant awareness of how you feel. When our body is hurting or tired, we are influenced to align our thoughts with the pain or fatigue in the body. However, to get to that "emotional state of well-being" discussed earlier as a definition of happiness, requires that we preserve thoughts that cause us to feel good.

When we are in the moment, we are present for bad influencers and we actively open ourselves up to good influencers; these may be different for everyone. Hearing birds chirping, seeing the radiant colors of flowers, watching the squirrels dancing around each other, viewing a sunrise and sunset, and witnessing all the wonders of nature inspire me. When I rush past myself, I don't notice this landscape and this lack of awareness over time influences my conscious and subconscious thoughts negatively.

Joy is a higher happiness that touches a deeper level of personal sensitivity, and inspires a warm feeling that nurtures the soul. There is a TV commercial that exemplifies this condition with a pig named Maxwell holding a toy propeller on a stick outside a moving vehicle, and as the wind spins the propeller, he screams WEEEEEEE... with animated enthusiasm. Every time I see that commercial, I believe there is nothing else that pig would rather do than speed briskly through winds to spin that propeller. That is an example of the miraculous joy I'm speaking of when you are feeling your greatest joy offered by the Spirit in small moments.

Another pleasurable moment that comes to mind is several years ago watching my sons sleeping when they were infants. Their adorable nature was accentuated with closed eyes and soft folded skin while breathing quietly and rhythmically with tiny hands clinched tightly; and with a soft touch on a palm would open just enough to grip my finger. That deep soul level feeling is created every time I think about it and is timeless.

To me joy is also watching kids uninhibited on the playground chasing each other around and around, and interacting in a manner that exhibits the same rotational orbits of planets in our universe. It is a surprising awareness to realize this and contemplate our eternal spirit nature – no greater joy! In *material* form we balance dualism with *meek strength*, while understanding the emotional pendulum will continue to swing, but we are to endure with patience and joy. Socrates once stated: "the secret of happiness, you see, is not found in seeking more, but in developing the capacity to enjoy less."[53] True wisdom is recognized mentally and felt emotionally.

Happiness and its advanced counterpart joy, are emotional vibrations transmitted on a higher level frequency than fear, frustration,

---

[53] Goodreads, Socrates Quotes http://www.goodreads.com/quotes/282137-the-secret-of-happiness-you-see-is-not-found-in

anxiety, jealousy, shame, etc. I have frequently observed that my cell phone transmits radio waves more effectively through glass than through brick. When we choose to close ourselves off to truth, we are in fact choosing to raise a brick wall.

When we open ourselves up to continuous happiness by allowing our emotions to whistle loudly with hypersensitivity permeating the *material* stuff in our bodies and external atmosphere, the effect is a magnetism that bonds with all matter on that frequency; the aura of attraction. I need to focus daily on recreating the necessary thoughts and emotions to manifest the results I expect to occur by faith. I do this by telling God my sincere thoughts (praying), calming my mind and listening for answers (meditating), exercising and drinking lots of water to rid the body of toxins (cleansing negative energy), and observing if fear has something valid enough to pay attention to (emotional awareness).

Laughing and smiling are very important as they release bio-chemicals for relaxation, boost our immune system, and increase blood flow to our heart. Since I seem to attract people with a great sense of humor, I'm puzzled that I'm widely perceived by some to be serious and unapproachable. Comedic entertainment is a favorite pastime of mine and I've learned to pay attention to smiling a bit more. Even when my thoughts are telling me I'm not happy my body still thinks I am.

Near the *edge of the beginning of my journey* in 2008, I explored ways for improving my happiness by returning to church, getting in touch with people I had grown apart from, praying routinely, working on my confidence, developing breathing techniques for material-spiritual alignment, reading books for personal development, and many other conscious activities. But I was still missing a piece of the puzzle to put all this together, since I still had not reached the personal satisfaction and happiness I was reading about.

That's when in 2010, I stumbled onto a trail of books on ancient literature, philosophy, and religion that sent me thousands of years back to English interpretations of writings in Sumerian, Egyptian, Akkadian, Greek, Mayan, Chinese, and many other languages. "Mine eyes" were opened to Truth I didn't know existed. And I, subsequently, became enraged that these materials weren't brought to my attention before then. Later I discovered that everything occurs according to purpose and that time in my life was appropriate for my newly inspired soul perception. Let me be clear that I needed to do this to discover my truth and so, the *pathway* for others may be different. Some people may not find joy in reading thousand-page books!

The puzzle piece I recognized was missing for me was the origin of scriptures we recognize as the Bible and the historical interpretations leading all the way up to the King James versions. There would have been no way for me to digest today's Biblical scriptures without processing the meanings of older writings. Now when I read the Bible, I understand why it is the greatest book of all time with eternal implications for humanity. Furthermore, I have a little more understanding of why some of the original books were separated from or not included in it at various periods in times past.

In this age when access to information is virtually unlimited, we continue to believe that certain information is prohibited because our leaders have told us so. Since human beings are fallible or prone to failing, consistently, how can we be so sure they are telling us the truth? I achieve intense levels of happiness and satisfaction by reading all kinds of information for myself first and then discussing what I've learned. However, that may stir controversy and fear and we certainly can't have disagreement in a civil society. "Yes we can!"

Several years ago, I was given a translated Hebrew version of the Artscroll Weekday Siddur, which is a Jewish prayer book. In 1991, while in the Army before the 100 hour assault during Operation Desert Storm, I visited an Islamic mosque in Saudi Arabia and was offered a Quran. Since I was raised a Christian in a Baptist Church was I supposed to refuse to accept or read these books with an openness to learn, which makes me happy?

Since many of our religious traditions have become so intertwined over thousands of years, I've found that all the major religious teachings across the world have at least one major belief in common. They worship One Divine Spirit as the Creator. In Islam, the term Muslim is an Arabic description for one who submits to the "One eternal and transcendent God." There are differences in practices, perspectives, and culture but where our ideologies intersect is very important. If we never agree on anything else, we should acknowledge that reality and share wisdom to bridge the historical divide.

The Jewish God is written as "...*our God, King of the universe...*" in the Siddur, and its prayers seek to unify the Name of God in perfect unity. Since God is Perfect without blemish, these prayers would not be referring to the "unification" of God or His Name literally. The union sought here is the "unification" of the separate pieces of Consciousness we each, individually, express to accomplish God's Divine Plan.

For instance, just like a train that travels on a single track in one direction and allows passengers to get off and on at specific stops, we all proceed with our Gifts as different expressions of the One True Mind. The train represents God's Consciousness, as we journey to our various equally important destinations with different roles, responsibilities, stops, and starts. However, we are all travelling together in the same direction toward Divine Perfection.

This may be a point of contention for some, but if you believe that God is outside of you controlling your destiny, then you implement "free will" in a manner that coincides with that belief system. Consequently, your life in *material* form will be the expression of that belief perspective. If you believe that God set the wheels of universe creation in motion in advance, according to established Laws and reaction energies, then you activate "free will" by getting on the *path to your inheritance.*

These interpretations of Divine Providence exist in Catholic, Jewish and Lutheran faith traditions, and have several degrees of variation expressed in their theology. But on a need-to-know basis, I wanted to dissect, comprehend, and streamline this knowledge to continue to grow my soul.

As I understand it, everything that occurs in our vast universe is in accordance with the Will of God. Also the provision for our lives known as Divine Providence is under His complete sovereignty. God's Will governs like an intricate computer programming language or "script" with inspirational opportunities and mysteries that continue to unfold over time toward Divine Perfection. I don't see a need to separate Divine Providence interpretations from each other, as I believe they all are true and intersect at very important points. If God's Perfect Will involves everything in creation from beginning to infinity in our *material* and *spiritual* realities, then His Will includes the creation beginning, creation preservation, and divine intervention in all ways possible – and impossible.

There is a spiritual idea or vision inside everyone of us that I refer to as the "blueprint" for our existence. I've discovered through my experiences offered here that only we, as individuals can see the details of our inner idea as they are etched in the fabric of our material *self*. Have you ever tried to convey an untested idea that you were seriously considering because you clearly saw its accomplishment in your mind? And the immediate response from a friend or relative was, "that's crazy!" Well there goes another potential breakthrough for humanity unrealized!

Throughout history up to about 1865, doctors and healthcare officials didn't regard cleanliness as a public health concern while caring for patients. Many patient deaths happened because contagious bacteria was spread by the medical care staff. Since there had been no consensus reached on a germ theory of disease, hospitals continued to observe the erroneous scientific opinions of the times.

In 1847, Dr. Ignaz Semmelweis, a Hungarian physician discovered that hand-washing, immediately, stopped the spread of deadly contagious diseases. He publically shared his research with doctors and medical care-givers and the discovery was greeted with hostility by the medical community. He spent 14 years developing his ideas and even wrote a book based on his findings, but the book received poor reviews and his research was again rejected. In 1865, he suffered a nervous breakdown and was committed to an insane asylum where, ironically, he soon died from a blood infection. [54]

That same year Joseph Lister, who seriously regarded Semmelweis'

---

[54] http://inventors.about.com/library/inventors/blantisceptics.htm

research began spraying a carbolic acid solution during surgery to kill germs. Although Lister's advances furthered the cleanliness debate and the medical community eventually adopted scrupulous hand-washing, he recognized and stated: "without Semmelweis, my achievements would be nothing."[55] I'm compelled to believe that if Lister had not demonstrated enough courage and resolve to continue pursuing the importance of cleanliness in medical care, thousands more people would have died over many more decades. And today we shudder at the thought of doctors and dentists approaching us during a visit before washing their hands; and this dramatic change occurred only about 150 years ago.

How many of us are still sitting on the sidelines of life in misery waiting for others to agree with the idea or vision that offers us an energetic happiness by merely thinking about it? If you've never heard this before, let my journey assure you that if your idea is sound by way of helping people, contributing good value to society, and being economically sustainable, no one else you know is able to see it clearly but you. Les Brown, world renown motivational speaker and author has about a thousand different quotes on this very thing but the one that sums up my belief about our *material* responsibility is this: "If you take responsibility for yourself you will develop a hunger to accomplish your dreams."[56]

Even though we are each commissioned for the pathway of our exclusive journey, we must choose to accept our anointing with eyes toward the goal, and our inner ear open to the Spirit. Our Divine Creator's Timetable in eternity isn't subject to the same limitations of a finite human experience in our *material* world. I believe that if we miss or choose not to accept our divine inheritance, the unfulfilled objectives of our purpose are extended for hundreds and potentially thousands of years until the time is true again for those pathways to intersect with divine intent. Contrary to popular belief there are no accidents or coincidences; there is only conscious and subconscious

[55] Ignaz Semmelweis: Medical pioneer persecuted for telling the truth: https://creation.com/semmelweis

[56] http://www.brainyquote.com/quotes/authors/l/les_brown.html

idea manifestation – creation. God's Plan must be fulfilled.

"But do not forget this one thing, dear friends: With the Lord a day is like a thousand years, and a thousand years are like a day. ⁹ The Lord is not slow in keeping his promise, as some understand slowness. Instead he is patient with you, not wanting anyone to perish, but everyone to come to repentance." (2 Peter 3:8-9, NIV)[57]

God has called each one of us to do something extraordinary here on earth according to the purpose for which we were born to explore and discover. I'm in no position to know, however, if we can achieve our own versions of success without actively worshipping God. But I'm convinced without conclusive evidence that we can never achieve our tallest dream without God's active involvement since it represents our true purpose and highest calling. Furthermore it is the only path for repeatedly bumping into joy that we often recognize, but don't realize we need and want more than anything for ourselves.

The purposeful "blueprint" that is written in us to accomplish is interpreted by the Spirit which leads us in exploring its content and meaning for a specific application. To me this concept is related to the "unseen" truth that is recurring in Biblical scriptures that speak of the Eternal Promise of God. An idea is eternal because it has not yet, unfolded in our physical world as a *material* presence and continues to live in the One Mind with no beginning or end. There are too many issues, circumstances, and problems that we encounter personally, and witness daily, for each of us to overlook that we have a *material* solution for a specific and problematic mystery in our lives.

I'll even go a bit further by asserting this: the primary reason that a problem persists in our lives and has created anxiety, depression, and maybe even despair is because we already have the answer key and refuse to use it to unlock and open the door to our truth, which leads to our inheritance.

But how can I possibly know this to be truth? Please continue

---

[57] New International Version (NIV), 2 Peter 3:8-9

reading and I believe you will uncover a puzzle piece that awaits, and will open a door to your soul that makes the statement above clear.

This was an area of confusion for me, as I observed people speaking of faith and lacking the *material* or physical presence of faith that must accompany faithfulness, or it is merely an idea. All life has purpose, and our existence on earth at this time in human history is to unfold the blueprint that is unique to us.

"For I know the plans I have for you," declares the LORD, "plans to prosper you and not to harm you, plans to give you hope and a future."[58]

Imagine for a moment where would we be as a global society without the purposeful ideas and work of the following innovators, and many others:

- Alexander Graham Bell was a scientist, inventor, and engineer who is credited with inventing the first practical telephone in 1876.
  - **Innovations:** additional inventions include work in optical telecommunications, hydrofoils, and aeronautics and became one of the founding members of the National Geographic Society in 1888.[59]

Quote: "What this power is I cannot say; all I know is that it exists and it becomes available only when a man is in that state of mind in which he knows exactly what he wants and is fully determined not to quit until he finds it."[60]

- Dr. Charles Drew was a medical doctor and surgeon whose ideas revolutionized the medical profession, saved many lives, and helped fight racism in the 1930s.
  - **Innovations:** started the idea of a blood bank and system for long-term preservation of blood plasma.[61]

Quote: "I feel that the recent ruling of the United States Army and

---

[58] New International Version (NIV), Jeremiah 29:11

[59] http://en.wikipedia.org/wiki/Alexander_Graham_Bell

[60] http://www.brainyquote.com/quotes/authors/a/alexander_graham_bell.html

[61] http://www.enchantedlearning.com/inventors/black.shtml

Navy regarding the refusal of colored blood donors is an indefensible one from any point of view. As you know, there is no scientific basis for the separation of the bloods of different races except on the basis of the individual blood types or groups."[62]

- George Washington Carver was a scientist, educator, humanitarian, and former slave whose research and product discoveries saved Southern agriculture in 19th century.
  - **Innovations:** developed crop rotational methods for conserving nutrients in soil and discovered hundreds of new uses for crops such as the peanut, which created new markets for farmers.[63] He pioneered a mobile classroom to bring his lessons to farmers called the "Jesup wagon," advised President Theodore Roosevelt on agricultural matters, was sought internationally for his scientific expertise, and was made a member of the British Royal Society of Arts. He also wrote a syndicated newspaper column and toured the nation and white Southern colleges for the Commission on Interracial Cooperation.[64]

Quote: "No individual has any right to come into the world and go out of it without leaving behind him distinct and legitimate reasons for having passed through it."[65]

- Henry Ford was founder of the Ford Motor Company in 1903, and was first to mass produce automobiles and to make them affordable for the general public.
  - **Innovations:** established the highest industry employee pay, implemented employee benefits and employment policies for ex-convicts and people with disabilities, and offered workplace educational facilities including an English Language School for immigrant employees onsite.[66]

---

[62] http://todayinsci.com/D/Drew_Charles/DrewCharles-Quotations.htm

[63] George Washington Carver: https://www.history.com/topics/black-history/george-washington-carver

[64] http://www.biography.com/people/george-washington-carver-9240299?page=2

[65] http://www.brainyquote.com/quotes/authors/g/george_washington_carver.html

[66] http://corporate.ford.com/our-company/heritage/heritage-news-detail/650-henry-ford

Quote: "Obstacles are those frightful things you see when you take your eyes off your goal."[67]

- Lewis Howard Latimer was an inventor and member of Thomas Edison's research team called "Edison's Pioneers" in 1918.
  o **Innovations:** improved the newly-invented incandescent light bulb by inventing a carbon filament, introduced the first toilet used in trains, and developed a forerunner of the air conditioner.[68]

Quote: "We create our future, by well improving present opportunities: however few and small they be."[69]

- Mother Theresa was a Roman Catholic nun, who devoted her life to serving the poor and destitute around the world, and was awarded the Nobel Peace Prize in 1979 for her selfless work.
  o **Innovations:** started "The Missionaries of Charity" in Calcutta, India to help the poorest people and to offer a home for people to die with dignity. These missions have grown to over 700 operating in over 130 countries and the scope of work has expanded to include orphanages, hospices for terminally ill patients, and efforts to assist the homeless and people affected with AIDS.[70]

Quote: "Not all of us can do great things. But we can do small things with great love."[71]

- Isabella Baumfree was a charismatic lecturer, abolitionist, and women's rights activist, who escaped slavery and gave herself the name Sojourner Truth in 1843.
  o **Innovations:** became the first black woman to win a court case against a white man to recover her son, who had been illegally sold into slavery.[72] Delivered her most famous speech entitled *Ain't I a*

---

[67] http://www.brainyquote.com/quotes/authors/h/henry_ford.html
[68] http://www.enchantedlearning.com/inventors/page/l/latimer.shtml
[69] http://todayinsci.com/L/Latimer_Lewis/LatimerLewis-Quotations.htm
[70] http://www.biographyonline.net/nobelprize/mother_teresa.html
[71] Ibid.
[72] http://en.wikipedia.org/wiki/Sojourner_Truth

Woman? at the Women's Convention in Akron, Ohio in 1851.[73] Met with President Lincoln in 1864 to discuss the nexus between the inferior legal status of African Americans and women in general; and remained in Washington to help the war effort by collecting supplies for black regiments serving in the Union army. Joined the National Freed-men's Relief Association to help former slaves find jobs and homes, and presented a "Negro State" proposal to Congress, which failed to achieve the necessary interest for consideration.[74]
Quote: "The Spirit calls me, and I must go."[75]

The famous visionaries previously mentioned paved the way for subsequent generations in society to build on top of their accomplishments. What is that "inner voice" nudging you to accomplish? I'm confident that we are much happier beings when we freely choose to play our purposeful role in the *material* world, since it naturally aligns with a vision that advances our values, talents, and insights in accordance with *meek strength*. Every decision the Spirit leads us to make interacts with the specific outcomes of other meek-strong visionaries in universal harmony according to the Divine Script. However, we must activate the compulsory openness to receive the free gifts of the Spirit and to access the internal "software" God preinstalled in us to accomplish His Purpose for our lives. Discover your truly joyous life!

Bottom line: joy is recognized on the pathway to uncovering our divine purpose, as a search for meaning drives an emotional balance that is welcome in all occasions.

---

[73] http://en.wikipedia.org/wiki/Ain%27t_I_a_Woman%3F

[74] The Free Dictionary, Sojourner Truth, http://legal-dictionary.thefreedictionary.com/Isabella+Van+Wagener

[75] Sojourner Truth: https://www.sojournertruth.com/

"I hold it true, whate'er befall;
I feel it, when I sorrow most;
'Tis better to have loved and lost
Than never to have loved at all."
– Alfred Tennyson

PART FOUR
What's Love Got to Do With it?

"If I speak in the tongues of men and of angels, but have not love, I am a noisy gong or a clanging cymbal. And if I have prophetic powers, and understand all mysteries and all knowledge, and if I have all faith, so as to remove mountains, but have not love, I am nothing. If I give away all I have, and if I deliver up my body to be burned, but have not love, I gain nothing." (Corinthians 1:13, ESV)[76]

Love is all that matters! A portion of our journey toward our inheritance is spent on a *path* to recognize and meet who we are and where we fit in the Divine Plan. I believe when we discover that we are much more than a physical body through Divine Intelligence of the Spirit, fear lowers his volume and our soul grows to establish connections to everyone and everything in our *material* world; an agape love.

We may look for opportunities to explore a kinship among other

---
[76] English Standard Version (ESV), Corinthians 1:13

souls, who may be friends and relatives; a phileo or brotherly love. The Song of Solomon in Biblical text goes into erotic detail about eros love, which is a sexual love in the context of marriage. Did I just say that sexual love is mentioned in the Bible?

Our ancestors before written language were already aware of a "living soul" *material* substance used as a knowledge system that learns through a shared human experience. The soul of the earth grows in density through a collective human consciousness expressed as our daily experiences, and represents the One True Mind of God.[77] This One Consciousness is interwoven into the "fabric" of the universe and is connected to the soul of the earth through a clear, subtle and electromagnetic substance known as "ether" (aether).[78] The existence of ether has been, passionately, debated for hundreds of years by scientists and theorists because experiments were unable to, adequately, account for the material.[79]

However, the chemistry of all natural elements such as air and fire require a "medium" of interaction with each other to make it all work for us. In other words, the medium that transmits sound on earth is air. The medium that transmits our thought and emotional vibrations throughout our seen and unseen universe is ether. Ether permeates everything in the cosmos and acts as a conductor of acoustic vibrations according to Dr. Gautam Chatterjee, a renowned historian of Indian Heritage.[80]

This eternal element transmits repeating occurrences of air pressure in the form of wave frequencies generated by our thoughts across infinite space.[81] Ether also allows us to receive the supernatural intervention responsible for the creation of our dream in the *material*

---

[77] Gregg Braden, *The Divine Matrix:* http://www.bing.com/videos/search?q=Gregg+Braden%2c+The+Divine+Matrix&qpvt=Gregg+Braden%2c+The+Divine+Matrix&FORM=VDRE

[78] The Aether is Pure, Conscious Oneness: https://divinecosmos.com/books-free-online/the-science-of-oneness/80-the-science-of-oneness-chapter-02-the-aether-is-pure-conscious-oneness/

[79] Michelson–Morley experiment in 1887

[80] Panchabuta or Five Elements: http://www.ibiblio.org/gautam/hind0003.htm

[81] Ibid.

world as long as we're open to it. What an exhibition of God's Love! Our thoughts, words and emotions vibrate the cosmic fabric of three-dimensions of space and one-dimension of time, and the Divine Creator authorizes the physical expressions of our requests in *material* reality.

Thousands of years ago ancient scientists and philosophers taught and wrote about these experiences that we are only now able to observe with the use of new technologies. About 400 years before the era of Christ, the great Plato presented the idea that there must be a fifth element beyond earth, wind, fire and water. The experiments of the time were missing an atomic variable to account for unexplained occurrences, and the idea of ether was asserted and is now more openly accepted. More contemporary names for ether are the Divine Matrix, the Field, and the Mind of God among others but its existence in our reality remains both a marvel and mystery.

According to Dr. Hans Jerry's Cymatics (sacred geometry), everything is comprised of ether—visible and invisible, and this substance allows sound vibrations to create our universe. See a demonstration of how sound changes the formation of matter at http://www.youtube.com/watch?v=vFRtjZ3NrqM.[82] The only difference between "ethereal" substances such as energy and matter is form. Contrary to popular belief there is no empty space. Something is always there as we exist in a sea of active potential and latent energy particles that organize according to the expression of sound! As it is written in Romans 8:39, (KJV):

"Nor height, nor depth, nor any other creature, shall be able to separate us from the love of God, which is in Christ Jesus our Lord."

This natural metaphysical (beyond physics) condition reassures me that I am, totally, surrounded by God's Unconditional Love at all times. How extraordinary is the reality we live in? God reminds us in Matthew 11:30 that if we have enduring faith His burden is light, and so the gifts of the Spirit will carry us because He loves us.

"In this the love of God was made manifest among us, that God sent his

---

[82] Cymatics: Sacred Geometry Formed by Sound http://www.youtube.com/watch?v=vFRtjZ3NrqM

only Son into the world, so that we might live through him. In this is love, not that we have loved God but that he loved us and sent his Son to be the propitiation for our sins. Beloved, if God so loved us, we also ought to love one another. No one has ever seen God; if we love one another, God abides in us and his love is perfected in us." (1 John 4:9-12, ESV)[83]

We are directly connected to all matter in our physical universe. And we are spirit and wonderfully made in the image of God serving at His Pleasure. I am reminded by recurring global events that we have much work to do in our physical existence, as the destiny of humanity is, inextricably, linked with the destiny of our earth. And our earth appears to be sick. As *material* and *spiritual* beings connected to every living and nonliving thing in our *material* world, we have a precious responsibility to love and support Mother Earth.

"*God blessed them and said to them, 'Be fruitful and increase in number; fill the earth and subdue it. Rule over the fish in the sea and the birds in the sky and over every living creature that moves on the ground.'*" (Genesis 1:28, NIV).[84]

If God is Love, Jesus Christ is Love, and we are made in His Image, then it follows, logically, that we are expressions of Love in human form. Accepting this reasoning should encourage us to make immediate and appropriate changes in our *material* lives. The Bible, science, and the organic compounds in our human bodies reveal that earth gave birth to the natural environment we originated from. Under the Providence of God, we are charged with caring for the Mother of Humanity, as she is important for our survival.

I surprise myself these days by joining the chorus of those who are sounding the alarm about a collective need to slow down, and take a look at our human condition. I don't mean to give the impression as if I'm swaying to the lyrics of John Lennon's song *Love*, holding

---

[83] English Standard Version (ESV), 1 John 4:9-12
[84] New International Version (NIV), *Genesis 1:28*

flowers, and wearing a dashiki. But I have become, increasingly, more troubled by the exploitation of our human and mineral resources for more corporate profits. These days there are more eyes to view such crimes and sometimes, we react to them like an episode on "reality" TV. As an undergraduate in Political Science I'm reminded, repeatedly, the first purpose of network news is to entertain. I got that answer wrong on a test once.

Ruling over all life on the planet, in the context used in Genesis 1:28, means that we take care of Earth and her inhabitants, so that she takes care of us. We are mutual beneficiaries of this care. Many of the energy challenges we face now were solved over 100 years ago through research and theoretical breakthroughs.

Today there are quiet developments of these century old ideas, but since our primary focus is applied to extracting all the "black gold" preserved underground there is not enough money or attention to spread to other workable alternatives. Nikola Tesla, an inventor, engineer and physicist was responsible for many of the discoveries in electricity and unconventional energy in the 19th century that are only now being applied as alternatives to our carbon energy dependence. Whether it happens because of individuals or, collectively, in the U.S. and around the globe, wherever our attention and focus are directed is where the *material* creation occurs.

The great George Washington Carver, an agricultural chemist, botanist, inventor and much more, found 300 uses for peanuts, and developed a crop rotational method that revolutionized southern agriculture.[85] GWC chose to use his "powers" of genius and invention to grow the soul of humanity – *meek strength*.

He made a conscious decision to make little money from his inventions, and only patented three of his ideas. His response was "God gave them to me. How could I sell them to someone else?" When we are confident in, committed to, and appreciative of our true purpose in this life, it is expressed as brilliance. And when we care for others more than we care about *material* wealth – that's love!

---

[85] http://www.biography.com/people/george-washington-carver-9240299

The earth supplied us with cotton and carbon for our human consumption for thousands of years, and we have, since found profitable and sensible plant fiber and blend alternatives to cotton for commercial use.[86] However, we are still heavily reliant on carbon energy for our daily use because it is an obvious solution, there is still more in the ground, and there are more profits to be earned. But at what costs? We are born with One Soul that must continue its progress toward Divine Perfection, and our addictions to profitable inefficiencies diminish us, as the quality of our lives suffer over time. What do we love?

Lord Alfred Tennyson, who was the national poet of England in 1850, authored the opening stanza at the beginning of *Part Four* as part of his poem, entitled *In Memoriam A.H.H.* Although I had always attributed this portion of the poem to a romantic love, Tennyson wrote these lines in remembrance of his friend Arthur Henry Hallam, who had died of brain trauma.

This poem is many pages long and speaks profoundly and intimately of the Oneness of God, which includes birth, learning and truth, light and darkness, faith and tribulation, beauty and love, and of course death. At this time and place on my *path*, I'm more certain now than when I began writing this journal that our role and purpose here in the *Land of Oz* is to love immensely; be loved thoughtfully; and to acknowledge and praise Love as a True expression of God's Divine Plan.

Bottom line: True Love manifests as harmony among thought, emotion, and feeling that is freely offered to others as a result of acknowledging God's Presence in all good things, including ourselves.

---

[86] Wanted: Sustainable, Cheap Alternatives to Cotton: https://www.fastcompany.com/1708845/wanted-sustainable-cheap-alternatives-cotton

"God knows us all too well to demand perfection of us.
Why would God set us up for failure, establishing a standard
none of us could meet?"– Harold S. Kushner

PART FIVE
We Are Fearfully and Wonderfully Made

I had never, truly, believed that I was good enough and, totally, equipped with everything necessary to fulfill my true purpose – not until only a few years ago. I couldn't get from here to there with the chorus that was singing that song. Furthermore, I was looking around to find people I could relate to, who were shiny with purpose and joyful like my grandfather. That would have made my walk a bit easier.

In 1980, I really got to know my grandfather, Tanner Pannell, by observing his daily routine and style that radiated a youthful vitality that was extremely alive and reborn on a daily basis. At this time, he was already 70 years young and his reputation for energy and well-being was renowned and celebrated for hundreds of miles. I knew it was something special back then, and I was experiencing it every day. Even in hindsight I'm still amazed at how he expressed greatness, daily, in the simplest ways.

I inherited an important piece of the Elkhorn community legacy and estate left by Tanner and Ethel Pannell established after the Depression Era, during the tumultuous periods of segregation in the 20th century. Elkhorn, located in a tucked away parcel of southwest Virginia at the intersection of Leda and East Elkhorn Road produced several generations of African-American families that actively participated in the farming and livestock industries.

This was during the "golden age" of family-centered communities with blended and extended families in almost every household for miles. The men earned a living in the scorching heat of the summer and during the merciless conditions in winter. Many of the women were college educated and were teachers of their children and community as they cooked, cleaned, and "kept house." The legacy and estate I inherited had nothing to do with monetary wealth or privilege. It has everything to do with the honor and respect bestowed to my grandparents, as entrepreneurs and proprietors of *Pannell's Grocery*, during a time when family and community were seamless. This was not the beginning of the Elkhorn story; it's just the portion of the story that is closest to my journey.

It's funny how we only remember snippets of our childhood that appear out of nowhere and lead us to an unexpected moment of either profound gladness or sadness. It's as if we have no power over our emotional memories, which are either too romantic or too dismal, since there doesn't seem to be any mediocre recollections that leave an impression.

There are times when circumstances have keys to the vault with our dusty memoirs stored away and the door swings wide open to reveal who we were at a certain time and place. In our *material* world all knowledge is cumulative, as a college professor once taught me and assembles together like a Lego construction with large and small pieces interlocking to make sense of colors and shapes. There is no separate knowledge or experience.

Everything we learn contributes to the whole of experience. The Mind is infinite – without beginning or end, and is communicating with us all the time whether we are paying attention or not. When we are open and aware of our-*selves*, we are able to select our memories from an unlimited Mind "buffet," which offers us a full serving of good thoughts and even better emotions.

When we are closed off to sunshine and "good vibrations" like a brick wall, those nefarious thoughts contributing to fear, anger, and frustration just show up! I choose often to reflect on the greatness of the Elkhorn community legacy, because I was planted and harvested there, and the soil is still rich with our heritage and future potential. It was not by accident that my experiences growing up there were, intensely, profound to me, as further reading will emphasize.

Tanner and Ethel were the full embodiment of Pannell's Grocery, as shoppers came to the store to buy "perishable" goods and socially interact with other neighbors separated by country miles. But customers were always greeted with a sincere smile and left with the eternal gifts of care, appreciation, and love. The Pannell's were the first residents in the community with a TV, so the store was an entertainment spot for all to share company in fellowship among friends, family, and adversaries.

They embraced everyone and no person ever left their presence without feeling an abundance of appreciation. I know this to be true because I've heard it from different people my entire life. Ethel Pannell died and returned to the Infinite Source at some period close to when my mom discovered she was pregnant with me. Maybe our eternal spirits passed each other as I traveled to the "silver" gateway of this *material* reality. I've always felt I knew her.

My parent's spousal relationship lasted long enough for me to arrive with my father's last name, and they separated a few years later. I'm the *material* product of an, extremely, passionate mother and an, immensely, rational father. I've found these character traits to be profitable, while acting in coordination, but they cancel each other out when applied separately.

Fortunately God thought it best that I possess these amazing attributes to walk my *path,* as I'm filled to the brim with both. When I was eight years old, my mom and pop agreed that I would live with my father most of the time, and they would share parental custody with frequent trips for me to visit my mother. It was a tremendously workable situation since I was exposed often to my mother's nurturing guidance, while living with the enduring presence of my father and grandparents.

During the summers, I would trade family locations to spend time with my mom's side of the family that included grandparents, uncles, aunts, and cousins. I recall the town of Norlina where I spent many hot summer days and cool dreamy nights to be reminiscent of a tribal village with a calm spiritual awareness, and a very tight-knit kinship dynamic. Nana and Papa, my mother's parents lived in a family-centered community similar in ways to Elkhorn but, also, different in as many ways. I was familiar with many of the people in the community, but my interaction with them was, primarily, driven by how my cousins and I would use their yards as a playground.

At the risk of turning this perceptual memory into an ancient cliché, during my stays in the Norlina village my cousins and I invented, as many games to play indoors and outside, as had existed for purchase in stores. Every neighborhood corner was a potential location to host a cookout, play kickball or start a badminton tournament. And that was in the daytime. As the sun went down, Nana's dinner preparation had concluded and Papa would assemble the homemade ice cream machine to churn banana soft serve – a flavor most retailers didn't offer then or now.

The tribal unit normally gathered in the front yard to watch the sunset and chat about random things. I realize now how important it is to stop, gather around, sit down, and discuss random things. This was how knowledge and wisdom was shared and passed down to each succeeding generation – before Facebook and Twitter. Let's stop for a moment and consider the communities we live in now. Could we be missing this essential family component of knowledge transfer today; and if so, is it possible for us to recapture?

Elkhorn was also filled with the spirit of love and compassion expressed through caring, kinship, character diversity and vigor. A "fearfully made" people with a keen awareness of God's Grace and Power that had been observed over decades and passed down to my father and to me. I was exposed to a rich *spiritual* tradition in this community that had adopted Pannell's Grocery store as the central meeting place in those early times. In rural towns where home and the workplace were often far apart, easy access to food, gas, and buying "on time" (credit) became primary staples of support from paycheck to paycheck.

While hanging out in the store from age eight to 18 and helping my grandparents, now Tanner and Susie his second wife, I had overheard the variety of issues that concerned older men and had witnessed their resolutions and dissolutions. I learned at an early age what could not have been learned or taught in public school; life is what you make it by the Grace of God.

I've always had a slight maturity that often confused me when I was a young child. Why did I know the answers to complex issues and challenges that seemed to trouble my peers, while I was growing up? I looked back at the quantity of hours, days, and years spent overhearing grown-up discussions and talking to elderly adults. And further, attracting friends three and four years older than me at every stage of growth from adolescence through my teenage years; therein lies the answer. My soul maturity had outpaced the age of my physical existence. And all this time I thought it was a natural talent!

We are "wonderfully made" for the journey we are supposed to take when we are open to that reality. At the store back then I had fun just sitting, quietly, among diverse groups of mature adults that, frequently, stopped by. These folks were teachers, ministers, farmers, law enforcement officers, elected representatives, miscellaneous professionals, pro athletes, business owners, and war veterans, just to name a few. The mixture of knowledge and experience I came into contact with on a, daily, basis undoubtedly encouraged me to see beyond my current rural setting.

Their discussions about religion, politics, social economics, and unrelated jargon permeated my soul and exposed me to the vastness of our world. And if they had realized how much I was listening, they may have told me to move on or obscured their language to confuse me. However, they never did that. I was permitted to sit and sometimes even participate when questions and conversations were directed to me. I had the greatest seat in the community. The front-row in the classroom of real life!

This early education was critical for a journey throughout my life, as it fostered a "knowing" in me, while making decisions, quickly, without second-guessing myself. I normally don't look back. My father has always emphasized how, deeply, rooted we are in our community and the importance of celebrating the goodness of heritage and the longevity of life many of our ancestors were blessed with in Elkhorn. In our early lives, we are, wholly, connected with the people closest to us in our social environment for a purpose.

Even when our individual experiences are perceived by us as extreme and difficult, upon release from the physical condition, a deeper search for meaning will uncover a mystery that offers liberation at some point. At that moment, we realize that our former agony has a potential to help hundreds or maybe even thousands of people. I believe our personal experiences, including instances of trauma may serve as the training ground for our life's journey toward our true inheritance. But we have to believe it to receive it.

We give up control of our individual lives, as embryos once our spirits become enmeshed in the *material* fabric of the One Soul at some point from conception to birth. The brief infancy and early childhood period in our physical lives is brimming with recurring exposure to early teachings and experiences perceived by us, as good and bad. For some the outcomes of these circumstances may result in expressions of emotional distress that I do not wish to make light of here.

One day, as we mature along the way, and even later into adulthood, we may need to seek help for the well-being that we are unable to achieve alone. While seeking professional help to guide us back to a place of acceptance and "openness," I find it plausible that God's healing occurs through various ways and means, in addition to direct healing. To think otherwise limits God's Power.

In order for me to have some understanding that God is All, I must conclude that He allows intervention by man in the form of therapists and physicians to heal, as we all are individual expressions of Him; and Jesus showed us the way. For Biblical technocrats that may believe that God only heals directly, I submit to you that Jesus used words, clay, and spit to heal the blind, which represented various "means" for healing. In the scriptures of Matthew 10:1, Mark 3:14-15, Mark 6:7, and Luke 9:1, Jesus trains his disciples for three years to heal and deliver the sick. All He asks is that we believe in the idea, and have faith about the outcome.

According to Freudian psychology and other research, our personalities are formed as early as five years old. Since God does not make mistakes, when we grow up in less than perfect circumstances, it was for a specific reason. It's up to us to "freely" make the decision to take personal action and discover it. I'm not able to speak for everyone but in hindsight, my challenges and failures have strengthened my resolve through the aches and pains of trial much more than my beautiful successes. However agonizing and even embarrassing, if my "washouts" contributed to a more balanced and reinforced soul, I am blessed to have experienced them.

We somehow need both good and bad experiences in preparation for our journey, as we are not otherwise able to accomplish His Will. The *pendulum of equilibrium* swings with remarkable opportunities for learning that are sometimes painful, but without adversity, we are still present in the Infinite Transcendence with no *material* existence.

"In the day of prosperity be joyful, and in the day of adversity consider: God has made the one as well as the other, so that man may not find out anything that will be after him." (Ecclesiastes 7:14, ESV)[87]

In the *material* world, we seek to balance the emotional pendulum with the gift of understanding that we have a specific purpose for existence that integrates with the Purpose for Humanity. It is written in *Psalms 117*, and many times throughout the Bible that God seeks praise from all nations and all peoples so *"the faithfulness of the Lord endures forever."*

Therefore, I'm led to believe that God seeks unity among all beings on earth to worship Him with the same manner of practice, as it is done in Heaven. We were created to worship Him and to fulfill His Unlimited Potential by re-discovering who we are, and being led by the Spirit on the *journey toward our true inheritance*.

By five years old the frame of our personality is, already, formed and progress toward character building continues as our beliefs, values, and experiences shape our worldview and contribute to a "wonderfully made" picture of us in the frame. When we are open to God's Purpose for our lives and the gifts of the Spirit, we balance difficult circumstances with love, self-control, faithfulness, optimism, kindness, and patience

---

[87] English Standard Version (ESV), Ecclesiastes 7:14

– the fruits of the Spirit.[88] Since Truth is unseen, the fruits of Truth exist as testimony or evidence of God's Goodness in our lives. When opened, these gifts transform our picture into a priceless work of art, because faithfulness in our true purpose is expressed as brilliance. Ephesians 2:10 (KJV) says:

"For we are His workmanship, created in Christ Jesus for good works, which God has prepared beforehand that we should walk in them."

It is written that God created us for the journey before we were born into this *material* reality. In other words, the journey was prepared for us, and we are prepared for the journey – touché!

Tanner or Top, as many close relatives referred to him, was a solid pillar of the community, whose spirit presence could light up a room. He had been in business so long the Virginia Alcohol Beverage Control (ABC) laws had changed. He was granted a "grandfather" provision to continue selling beer for consumption on the premises that was, only, reserved for restaurants that served cooked food. No other stores around had that type of proprietary flexibility.

Although the sale of alcohol was a very large portion of his business, if my grandfather believed a person had drunk too much, he would not continue selling alcoholic drinks to that individual. Furthermore, if he had gained knowledge of individuals engaging in unhealthy activities promoted by alcohol use in the community, he would have firm conversations with those people, individually, about their behavior.

I remember the embarrassed expressions on many faces as they, slowly, returned to their cars with their bags in hand. I even recall young men feeling apologetic before entering the store, and taking a few minutes to build up courage by talking to me before they entered, as if I could help. They knew what they had to endure before making a purchase from Top: tough love with a handshake and a promise to do better.

My grandfather never really surprised me, as I had grown to know

---

[88] Wikepedia: Fruit of the Holy Spirit http://en.wikipedia.org/wiki/Fruit_of_the_Holy_Spirit

exactly what to expect from him. If someone didn't believe in going to church, I knew how he would respond. If someone wasn't working a job somewhere, I knew how he would respond. If something needed a repair, he would always try to fix it himself often creating the need for a professional repair, immediately. He wasn't perfect and had only a little formal education, but he prayed consistently and acknowledged God in everything he did.

He knew he was a blessed man with less than a third grade education, a prosperous business, and was doing what he loved to do every single day. A life tilted to the unique talents of an individual that glows with an aura of happiness, and exemplifies health, love, and stability is the life I believe to be inspired by God. I wanted that!

Indeed, I've always had a vision for the type of life I wanted since I could clearly see me in it, but the bigger the job title I was promoted to and the more money I made, the emptier I felt inside. In this, I knew without any doubt that I needed to make a substantial life change.

I formed Pannell Enterprises LLC in 2011, while still working full-time in my public sector career. *PE LLC* was an idea born out of a tremendous respect for Tanner Pannell, whose life touched thousands of people and to me was deserving of a living memorial to honor past contributions with blessings toward the future in a similar way. I developed the company logo by enlisting my friends to do the artwork. They created a digital image of him using a real photo so the art would be a good physical representation of Tanner with his natural human features. Tanner Pannell's soul is with us and lives on.

We read about our earthly heroes in books and see them on TV without ever meeting them in person to get a glimpse of a true personality. I guess sometimes that may be for good reason, since our unlimited mind conjures up prettier pictures than a human being could ever live up to. Although imperfect, "Grandpop" personified an observable type of *meek strength* that welcomed others and left a grand impression. Along these contour lines, I developed a company with a social-economic mission to foster better communities by establishing better companies in them. I intended to establish businesses and investment opportunities in other entrepreneurial ideas that intersected with *PE LLC's* "socio-eco" purpose.

Social change is a natural progression toward perfection with mutual benefits established among our families, communities, institutions, and governments under the Providence of God. I'm sincerely troubled by the free-wheeling economy, poor environmental and social conditions, and unwillingness of many to witness these outcomes with a conscious awareness. We are the physical creators of this world, and we have, collectively, agreed to manifest these conditions.

Change is a constant occurrence in our world. But when we keep our heads buried and eyes shut in oblivion to the natural fluctuations of economic cycles in joblessness, income hardship, and financial instability, we ignore our *material* reality, which swings the *pendulum of equilibrium*. Human beings established this economic and political system under a "social contract," and we give our government representatives our permission to establish and enforce laws that are beneficial at times and sometimes oppressive.

Remember that not voting or participating in civic responsibilities is a conscious decision too. Since we, actively, participated at some point in the creation of the conditions in our lives or moved about without, consistently, observing the results of our actions, we are, certainly, capable of creating better lives with a clear vision and sound Mind. *"We are fearfully and wonderfully made"* to acknowledge God in all things and to take our steps onto the Divine Path that awaits us. In this portrait, we demonstrate *meek strength*.

My wife and I, frequently, remind our sons now ages 15 and 19 that they are "fearfully and wonderfully made" as expressions of our Divine Creator. With this honor and privilege, they should act like they are representatives of the Most High. In practice, this means to honor their parents by following instructions and doing their best in all activities. The results of doing our best don't always translate to being the best in our daily pursuits, but when we do our best we "feel" better.

Our sons are great students and good athletes, and we are confident it's because of Grace, and the consistent prod we give as a reminder to represent themselves in a manner that is pleasing to the King. When we work to do our best we are not seeking to compete with others or gratify our egos. We are seeking to please and honor God because each of our lives should exhibit the Greatness of God to "attract" and encourage others to take a walk to remember who they are.

But what happens when the *pendulum of equilibrium* in our lives swings with "reckless abandon" toward adversity causing a *material* and emotional setback? In the aftermath, we learn the shadows of doubt and fear have, promptly, arrived to erode our confidence in the fruits that have blossomed for years as expressions of joy, faith, patience, peace, and kindness. Doubt and fear are never late!

As these shadows darken the doorway we've left unlocked, we sometimes forget the Spirit has never left us and is still there with an extended hand waiting to offer the counsel we need to feel better. But yet again, we must be open to receiving it. During times of challenge, fear and adversity, God has, already, preinstalled the "software" for us to know that *A Psalm of David (Psalms 23, NIV)* is truth and repeating the following verses will chase away fear and doubt. The Light of Truth overwhelms the shadows of doubt and fear.

"¹ The LORD is my shepherd, I lack nothing. ²He makes me lie down in green pastures, he leads me beside quiet waters, ³ he refreshes my soul. He guides me along the right paths for his name's sake. ⁴ Even though I walk through the darkest valley, I will fear no evil, for you are with me; your rod and your staff, they comfort me. ⁵ You prepare a table before me in the presence of my enemies. You anoint my head with oil; my cup overflows. ⁶ Surely your goodness and love will follow me all the days of my life, and I will dwell in the house of the LORD forever."

If we are open to receiving the gifts of the Spirit, we display the fruits as well. Conversely, if there are no fruits – there are no gifts, or they are still waiting in the universal "queue" to be processed. I'm consistently reminded that these free gifts of wisdom, understanding, knowledge, fear of the Lord, etc. are accepted in accordance with the maturity level of our soul.[89] When each of us at different times in our lives decides to step out onto our anointed *path*, faithfulness blooms as

---

[89] Wikipedia: Seven Gifts of Holy Spirit http://en.wikipedia.org/wiki/Seven_gifts_of_the_Holy_Spirit

a fruit of wisdom. The degree of faith we have, individually, corresponds to the level of wisdom and understanding we have achieved through our *material* experiences.

When we learn to balance the *pendulum of equilibrium* in our lives by calming our emotions and submitting to the Will of God, we become masters of our will during challenges and trial. The soul grows and matures this way. Aristippus, a student of Socrates, once said "it is not abstinence from pleasures that is best, but mastery over them without being worsted."[90] One perspective of this philosophy may include that abstinence is "sacrifice" and creates feelings of lack. When we believe that we "do not lack and want nothing," we are free to open our-*selves* to what God has for us. By the Grace of God, we are led on the *path* using the gifts of the Spirit to identify and accept our Divine Inheritance.

Any person can be prayerful, pretty, and proud when our pendulum swings toward *material* bliss that arises in response to external stimuli. Emotional happiness is found on the opposite side of sorrow and is subject to erratic mood swings back and forth. Joy is a fruit of the Spirit that comes when we seek the free gifts described earlier. It is available during happy and troubled times when we are open to acknowledging it as a companion of faith.

The Universal Principle of Polarity reminds us often the emotional *pendulum of equilibrium* must swing from side to side in search of a balance that promotes understanding.[91] The foundation of learning is understanding, which is a gift of the Spirit. This is neither controversy nor a depressive state of existence. It is our *material* reality. Humanity has always been affected by the interactions of the Universal Laws of the cosmos since the *spiritual* Fall of Man. However, those who joyfully "reign" in our *material* existence are those who are led by the Spirit on *their journey toward their inheritance*. And yes, that's a demonstration of *meek strength*.

We are "fearfully and wonderfully made" because we were created to be in awe of and to have reverence for God with an overwhelming

---

[90] Great Thoughts Treasury *http://www.greatthoughtstreasury.com/abstinence/quotes-0*

[91] *The Kybalion*, by Three Initiates, (1912), http://www.sacred-texts.com/eso/kyb/kyb04.htm

sense of glory based on the work of many Hebrew scholars. If we are One Humanity in the material fabric of the cosmos and also individual aspects of the One Mind of God then we are "wonderfully made" because God Loves us both personally and universally.

We are different *material* expressions of the Divine Oneness shaping the matter of our world to reveal God's Plan. If King David believes and declares that he is "fearfully and wonderfully made" because he is the acknowledged king by God's Grace, he becomes just a mere example of meekness through his submission to God's Will, and praise to the Almighty for granting his divine inheritance. In Acts 13:22, the Apostle Paul is ministering to the men of Israel and says:

"After removing Saul, he made David their king. God testified concerning him: 'I have found David son of Jesse, a man after my own heart; he will do everything I want him to do.'"[92]

David in numerous Biblical scriptures exhibited obedience, adoration for God's Law and extreme faithfulness in pursuing the *path* to his ultimate destination, as the rightful heir to the throne of Israel. This also, exemplifies the character of any person after God's own heart; one who is faithful, God fearing and reveres the Law – one who has *meek strength*!

It's essential to the meaning of the Biblical saga to also, understand that King David was an adulterer and murderer but still had momentous favor with God. To me that is the true essence of the story. We are never good enough, faithful enough, or loving enough to earn God's Love and Grace – we can only be open to receiving it. When we freely choose to accept God's Love by taking the anointed *path* God has already prepared for us, we become the rightful heirs to our inheritance as well.

Today, September 23rd, I signed my first bulk food delivery agreement with a client for eight-months. God is Good! My purpose here is to offer client services with extraordinary value for people and communities while creating jobs and opportunities for investing in

---

[92] New International Version (NIV), Acts 13:22

people. Initially, I developed several business plans but started business operations with the plan that involved frozen food distribution since the industry was closed to competition with high barriers of entry including knowledge, information, experience, cost of specialized equipment, funding, etc. The high barriers of entry to do business in this industry also offer a competitive advantage for start-up companies like mine that identify ways to compete in narrowly focused areas.

Awareness of the Laws of Attraction assured me that I would attract the appropriate expertise I needed along the way, to help me develop the lines of business I'd already written a plan for, as long as, I was open to the opportunities. Being open during the journey means that my feelings are unguarded, and I allow myself to feel every emotion related to the decisions I make. I'm also, open to considering the infinite possibilities both small and tall with patience and gratitude.

Sunshine and cell phone signals travel through glass very easily, whereas brick walls shield both. Tearing the emotional obstructions down to feel all of the natural sensations of excitement, vulnerability and fear creates an awareness of how we feel at every moment, so we consciously adjust our thoughts on the fly. I'm confident that by aligning my thoughts and emotions with the high pitch vibrations of patience and gratitude, I attract other creative souls on those same emotional frequencies.

Harmonizing our thoughts on the frequency of good vibrations, consistently, is a struggle because we are often distracted by life's challenges and short-term opportunities. As our emotional *pendulum of equilibrium* oscillates with dramatic force, God seeks to offer us gifts both seen and unseen to further inspire our creations.

Just like getting a new toy, when I learn something new, exciting and life-changing, I read the instructions and try to apply it, exactly, as written to know if it really works. After reading several books on "attraction energies," as you might have guessed I put it to use right away! I added meditation sessions of at least a half-hour to increase my feelings of "openness and safety" in this newly found vulnerable condition.

Many of us feel like the show of vulnerability is a display of weakness, but as flawed human beings, people who see us every day are already aware of our weaknesses. It is when we act like they don't exist, we look awkward and disturbed. A show of vulnerability, consequently, displays a perception of knowing that we ourselves, are fallible and prone to failing, frequently. Therefore, a show of vulnerability is a display of strength in knowing who we are, and when we show vulnerability before God that is an exhibition of *meek strength*.

On the *path* to rediscovering who I am, has been exciting and humbling. I improved awareness that I was made to create and manifest ideas that express love, appreciation and joy. My current walk and intent is to help create easy and affordable methods for businesses and organizations to receive and transport cold and frozen foods for customer and employee convenience. My company is able to do this by installing frozen-food vending machines onsite and by transporting and delivering bulk food items. A second *PE LLC* company offers trailer rentals to individuals and small businesses who may need refrigeration for short-term and temporary storage.

When I have flowing thoughts of implementing those ideas, I feel encouraged to find additional ways and people to broaden the approach. So far I've launched two companies under Pannell Enterprises LLC that will do just that: Food Vending Solutions and Fridge On Wheels Rentals. My wife is instrumental in supporting me with her investments of time, money, and critical perspectives. Although there are others who encourage me including my mom, who gives me money every time I visit her, I'm wise enough to know that we must have reliable support from the closest person in our circle since "it takes two to make a thing go right." Evidence of this is shown in Matthew 18:19 (NASB):

"Again I say to you, that if two of you agree on earth about anything that they may ask, it shall be done for them by My Father who is in heaven."[93]

When two or more people agree on a common goal, the power of faith is magnified and God induces the Spirit to offer additional gifts that support our journey and allow us to be calm under pressure, in order to progress further on the *path*.

---

[93] New American Standard Bible (NASB), Matthew 18:19

This new business initiative and mission was too important to be left, totally, in my hands and I was led to experienced people with the expertise to assist me with developing my ideas in 2011. These people lived in other states including Colorado, Florida, and Ohio, and two of the individuals I didn't even meet until after a year of discussions over the phone and email.

Additionally, the gentleman that serves, as my current business mentor, is an experienced entrepreneur in his mid-70s. I don't believe a coincidence like this happened by accident. When our faithful activities are aligned with God's Magnificent Power, people will go out of their way to help us. While standing in grocery store lines with fewer items, people are often compelled to let me get in front of them and refuse to accept no, as my response.

One day while stopped on the interstate highway in idle traffic conditions on the way to a meeting with a client, a truck driver looked at the door decal on my truck and waved his hand to get my attention. He informed me that approximately five miles ahead there was an accident, and it would be better if I crossed in front of him to take the exit ramp as a detour. That truck driver saved me at least four hours on the highway that day, and he's probably the kind of guy that does this type of thing all the time. The Spirit had created the provisions for our paths to intersect, and I was able to proceed with no perceptual adverse impact.

Just as the impact of gravity is, easily, identified the powerful magnetic "attraction" forces are most influential when our vision is clear, and we understand that with faith we exhibit patience and gratitude in the face of difficulty. When we feel this inner peace "resolve," we are able to emote with confidence and commitment about our idea, and the cycle of positive feeling begins again and again with persistent, daily, optimistic thoughts.

I've struggled with patience my entire life, because I was burdened with a "wonderfully made" interpretation of the talents God gave me that existed to fulfill my own version of success. In my prolific version, we were supposed to drive our life with these talents, and at some point our ambitions and God's Purpose would meet. But I was already driving my life with my talents, and I was miserable, tired, and no closer to my dream than I was seven years ago. And another issue that, relentlessly, plagued me was: why were people with what I perceived to be less going on in their lives happier than me?

I had missed the boat for sustainable happiness, entirely, and wasn't even standing on the dock to get aboard. Since our inner feelings, truly, reflect our emotional well-being, I knew something was wrong with how I was feeling. However, I wasn't consciously aware of my true purpose for existing in the *material* world. We do not live here to create for our-*selves*. We are using our talents and passion to create for God's Purpose. We must humbly ask God for the contents of our true purpose, and if we're open to His Guidance, the Spirit leads us *to the edge of the beginning of our journey.*

Bottom line: humans were created with limited potential to worship the Infinite Power of God by being open to discovering our beauty and promise in His Purpose.

"Therefore I tell you, whatever you ask in prayer, believe that you have received it, and it will be yours." – John 5:31

PART SIX
The Power of Prayer

Father, I submit to Your Will, as I am nothing but an instrument that You play for Your Purpose. In Jesus' Name, Amen.

As I continue to document significant observations, during my thirteen week journey, I make no pretense to be an expert on religion, morality, prayer, or any other sacred traditions. However, I offer to all, who are willing to accept, a clear perspective for issues that have confused me throughout my life up to now. Prayer happens to be one of those mystifying issues that really should be more understood, if it improves our relationship with God. But many people, pastors, and practitioners disagree on what it is, and how we're supposed to do it. How can this be, if it's so important?

I believe it's human nature to disagree, and conflict can even be used to generate consensus, if all involved are open to a mutual resolution. But I don't accept that a relationship with God is difficult at all, since Jesus gave us the words to use and reasons during the Sermon on the Mount in Matthew 6:7-13 (KJV).

"⁷But when ye pray, use not vain repetitions, as the heathen do: for they think that they shall be heard for their much speaking. ⁸Be not ye therefore

like unto them: for your Father knoweth what things ye have need of, before ye ask him. ⁹After this manner therefore pray ye: Our Father which art in heaven, Hallowed be thy name. ¹⁰Thy kingdom come. Thy will be done in earth, as it is in heaven. ¹¹Give us this day our daily bread. ¹²And forgive us our debts, as we forgive our debtors. ¹³And lead us not into temptation, but deliver us from evil: For thine is the kingdom, and the power, and the glory, forever. Amen."

I've overheard many family members, who've said "prayer changes things" and I have intuitively always known that as well. Very often we believe things without knowing or we know things without believing. But the matter about prayer changing things is one thing I know and believe to be Truth. People are "free" to have their opinions about how prayer has either helped them or not, but I offer that our very existence to this day, and at this very moment is because of many, many prayers occurring 24-hours a day, every day.

There are many billions of people around the world praying about the same issues inherent in our human nature, which brings about harmony at critical times to humanity on Planet Earth and throughout our universe. Additionally, God offers us daily instances of Grace and Mercy by waking up the sun every morning, and swiping asteroids away from earth's orbit when they are on track to greet us from outer space. We are never good or faithful enough to earn God's Love. Thank You God that You offer it freely!

Prayer allows us to ask God for His Power to accomplish His Purpose. Jesus offers us insight into this Authority in Matthew 21:18-22 (NKJV) when the disciples show their disbelief in the Power that Jesus says is available to all who believe.

¹⁸Now in the morning, as He returned to the city, He was hungry. ¹⁹And seeing a fig tree by the road, He came to it and found nothing on it but leaves, and said to it, "Let no fruit grow on you ever again." Immediately the fig tree withered away.²⁰ And when the disciples saw it, they marveled, saying, "How did the fig tree wither away so soon?" ²¹ So Jesus answered and said to them, "Assuredly, I say to you, if you have faith and do not *doubt, you will not only do what was done to the fig tree, but also if you say to this mountain, 'Be removed and be cast into the sea,' it will be done. ^{22} And whatever things you ask in prayer, believing, you will receive."*

A prayer involves talking to God about everything, and to get the most out of this relationship we should "pray without ceasing." "Thank you Jesus for waking me up this morning; thank you Jesus for helping me get to work safely; thank you Jesus that I have a few dollars to eat today; thank you Jesus that nothing aches; and thank you Jesus that I can see, hear, touch and smell. Thank You Jesus that if none of those things are true, I still praise Your Name because I'm still alive and there is still something You want me to do."

^{16} *"Rejoice always; ^{17} pray without ceasing; ^{18} in everything give thanks; for this is God's will for you in Christ Jesus."* 1 (Thessalonians 5:12-19, NASB)[94]

Prayer for large and small things shows appreciation and gratitude in the midst of life circumstances going right and wrong. Evidence for the previous statement is in the Bible from front to back, but Luke 16:10 offers the following: *"He that is faithful in that which is least is faithful also in much..."* The display of appreciation and gratitude is faithfulness in action, and occurs as a powerful biochemical process in our bodies that radiates outward. God ultimately blesses us for how we feel, as our thoughts and emotions are present in the feeling. This primordial interaction within our bodies influences the surrounding environment or the soul of the earth. More explanation about this in the next *Part* of the journal.

Although our *Father knows what we need before we ask Him,* we must ask and believe we have already received it by faith, which is faithfulness in action. This is very important to comprehend because even though God has our lives and deaths already predetermined, He allows us to humbly request changes and variations in our lives that

---

[94] New American Standard Bible (NASB), Thessalonians 5:12-19,

have already been accounted for. There are not many instances of this "clearly" shown in the Bible, which tells me this may be a special request, but following is an excerpt about it in 2nd Kings. Faithful, Hezekiah, King of Judah, is on his deathbed and prays to God for Mercy.

¹ "In those days Hezekiah became ill and was at the point of death. The prophet Isaiah son of Amoz went to him and said, 'This is what the LORD says: Put your house in order, because you are going to die; you will not recover.' ² Hezekiah turned his face to the wall and prayed to the LORD, ³ 'Remember, LORD, how I have walked before you faithfully and with wholehearted devotion and have done what is good in your eyes.' And Hezekiah wept bitterly. ⁴ Before Isaiah had left the middle court, the word of the LORD came to him: ⁵ 'Go back and tell Hezekiah, the ruler of my people, This is what the LORD, the God of your father David, says: I have heard your prayer and seen your tears; I will heal you. On the third day from now you will go up to the temple of the LORD. ⁶ I will add fifteen years to your life. And I will deliver you and this city from the hand of the king of Assyria. I will defend this city for my sake and for the sake of my servant David.' ⁷ Then Isaiah said, 'Prepare a poultice of figs.' They did so and applied it to the boil, and he recovered." (2 Kings 20:1-7 NIV)[95]

Prayer changes things, if it is not yet clearly apparent. We must talk to God all the time, every day, and all day. This is perpetual prayer, or "praying without ceasing." Wherever our focus is – that is where our reality exists. If we aren't worshipping God, we are worshipping *some thing*. The sooner we know what it is, the more potential we have to be led to the *edge of our golden path* by the Spirit.

Truth is found in our daily "lingo" and dialogue, however, we don't really understand it as Truth, unless we are freely open to it. Most of the sayings and proverbs I've written in this journal, I've heard my entire life. However, I moved through various life phases clueless about how to apply the ancient principles to my life and, therein, lies a potential problem. Life is perceived and lived through the human

---

self, which matures through an individual soul that is connected to the One Mind (ether) that we all share in human form on earth. More, specifically, we are progressing through life as a single expression of God to discover our Divine Purpose, and to connect with other souls, in order to work in unity for a larger and more True Purpose.

As human beings in this lifetime, if we don't "freely" accept our anointed *path,* then we "freely choose" fear, doubt, depression, and other un-Godly attributes. This is the "free will" granted by God that we've all heard about. God, also grants exceptions, benefits, exclusions, opportunities, protection, favor, mercy, blessings, Love, second and third chances, health, purposeful success, wealth, and "anything" you ask; as long as you believe with every fiber of your being.

As human beings, we were created for worship. Science informs us that we are "energy" beings, since matter and energy are equal; remember $E=mc^2$? With continuous "focus," we are able to change the molecules of our bodies and bring into our physical environment whatever we choose. However, without a relationship with God our choices have limitations and are dangerous. With God, our choices are granted maximum potential. God intends to awe us in the process of living. It is written that we are "fearfully and wonderfully made," or made with the intent to be inspired to do the extraordinary things we were created for.

John Wheeler, who was a scientist and colleague of Albert Einstein, suggested that reality is created by observers and that: "no phenomenon is a real phenomenon until it is an observed phenomenon." He coined the term "Participatory Anthropic Principle" (PAP) from the Greek "anthropos", or human. Wheeler went further to say that "we are participants in bringing into being not only the near and here, but the far away and long ago."[96] Furthermore, we live and manifest our lives according to our beliefs and those beliefs change the *material* around us.

The evidence is clear and is presented here in "3-D": 1) we are part of a participatory universe; 2) it is a Biblical principle that we

---

[96] John Wheeler's Participatory Universe: https://futurism.com/john-wheelers-participatory-universe

must participate and follow our dream to fulfill our True Potential; and 3) science recognizes the previous observations preserved in ancient records that were translated in the 12th century: "That which is above is from that which is below, and that which is below is from that which is above, working the miracles of one." (The Emerald Tablet of Hermes, Holmyard 1923: 562).

I don't believe that most people in society don't want a better life, or are not working hard to achieve it. Just like I was confused about the process for achieving a good life because incomplete information is offered in too many places, others may be feeling the same way. Seeking God's Goodness in our lives may cause us to feel like His Time is competing with our work, family schedules and TV time, and that's because it is.

When we separate God from these normal routines, we compete for time in all these areas and we do not win if we compete with God. The key is to seek God while we do these things and ask for His guidance as we make decisions in these areas. Everything is God and we should constantly seek to unite the separate pieces of our lives under His Providence so they work for us instead of against us.

Access to unlimited amounts of random information is an area that we must regulate. We consume too much daily information and 80% of it we probably don't need, unless our job requires it. I'm down to about 5-10% of the news I used to read and watch, and refuse to view repeating episodes of the same. It's addictive and our subconscious mind picks it apart until it tastes something deliciously harmful to hang on to. The subconscious mind replays this "tidbit" of information over and over again until something surprising and disturbing manifests in our reality. And we think someone else did it to us!

Again, if we aren't worshipping God, we are worshipping *something*. *Any-thing* we consistently give our conscious and subconscious energies to is something we care a lot about or even love whether we are aware or not. The challenge is to know and understand what our subconscious mind is retelling us every single day. We meditate to silence our conscious mind, and listen to the more powerful subconscious mind because "what she says, goes."

Contrary to popular belief, prayer and meditation are natural partners and complete each other. Prayer is talking to God and meditation is the act of quietly listening to our-*self* and the inner voice of the Spirit, if we believe and open up our "vessel." Prayer and meditation sessions don't have to be conducted as long rituals. They should be developed as habitual practices that we perform throughout the day so that our attention constantly departs from unintentional habits – to what we intend to create in our lives.

Remember that we are created for worship and God offers us "free will" to come to Him on our own. This is a beautiful concept when you stop and think about it. Where else is there a deal like this? Our Creator offers Jesus to believe and observe as the Truth for "eternal life." And we consciously choose our own limited and adverse lives instead. The word "eternal" gives the impression that we need to die, in order to receive the Goodness of God. So why is it in our interest to turn toward God now, when there is so much of the world to get in to?

We are eternal beings draped in *material* "robes" we will remove upon death. The *material* of our bodies is finite but the *spirit* is eternal and transcendent. This observation conveys that our lives require a *balance* that serves both components of our true nature. Just like our subconscious mind, if we aren't actively feeding that unseen *spiritual* component, we are neglecting the most powerful "technology" of our-*selves*. This is equivalent to an elegant but empty picture frame sitting without a picture, and therefore, having no true purpose.

At this moment, while writing this I can only smile at the many times I walked away from accepting my anointed *path*. The *path* has always been leading me to forming a company and I knew it, and even told others many times. But I had "tasted" perspectives that may have been true for others on a different *path*, like "the economy is too bad to start a new business, the business idea is too new and unfamiliar, and never leave a secure job to do something that 80% of people fail in the first year."

Since every person alive is uniquely talented and qualified for their journey, we must be extremely careful in offering "advice" to others by observing our own biases. Believing that we are being helpful to others when we focus on the "realistic" negative aspects of a situation is a myth. A balanced perspective involves discussing the "realistic" positive aspects of the situation as well, and with both viewpoints, we are able to weigh the feasibility of any situation. The path can become long, difficult and hopeless when we begin a mythical journey.

Before offering any sort of advice, we should pray with the individual or remove ourselves, and pray alone to ask for the type of guidance that would be appropriate to offer. During moments like these, we are either facilitators of God's Wisdom, or proud administrators of *self-ish* estimation. This is one of those fork in the road scenarios when someone "really needs our advice" and we have to muster up enough audacity to know how to help. If people know me and they come to me for "advice," I will test them to see if they really want it by quizzing them on their own assumptions. If they fail the quiz with "I don't know" or "I don't care about that," they will either drop the subject or do more research and come back.

When people approach us with a certain level of interest for advice, the goal should be to guide them to their own decisions, and not to lean on any predeterminations we've made. We will never know the root cause of motivations or the circumstances that are leading people to make decisions because people speak from their first-person perspective only. We can never know the depth or breadth of the issue and so, our guidance will be marginal at best. For everyone involved, we must totally submit to the Spirit who will lead us to what we should say and how we should say it.

When I first began working full-time in my public service career, I was a management analyst at a small independent Federal agency. I wanted to get some good working experience where there were many attorneys because I had planned to request a letter of recommendation for law school. About three years and numerous Agency awards and recognition certificates later, I approached one of the highest officials in the Agency for a meeting and he agreed. In "Ian" fashion, I greeted this gentleman respectfully with my spoken and written resume. I knew exactly why I was there and he probably did too. However, I left his office that day unexpectedly feeling challenged and deflated. This gentleman had asked me the following questions: "where did I want to go to law school and what type of law did I want to practice?"

My response was that I didn't intend to practice law. I wanted to go to law school for the education and to use the credentials in other areas. That must have been enough to give the appearance of committing a "cardinal sin." The bottom-line was people only go to law school if they plan to practice law because that's the purpose of law school. There is no other reason for going through the "mental hazing" and the enormous financial burden unless you are going to put the training to use. Can you believe that? He was telling me the truth and I was offended by it.

I was offended for six months or more until one day it finally hit me. I was already midway in my civil service career and if I decided to practice law at a law firm, get a judge clerkship, or even work at a government agency, I would need to begin as an entry-level attorney. I thought: "by the time I finished a part-time law school program, I would be at least two levels higher in the civil service than I am right now. There's no way I'm going back to an entry-level start anywhere." Even though it took me a while to see the blessing in the discussion with the gentleman, I'm thankful now that he told me. I'm already over $100 thousand in student loan debt! Thank You God for that gentleman.

I watched my grandfather for many years praying every night on his knees before he went to bed. He praised Jesus throughout the day, impressed upon others how important He was for everything and even yelled His name at times to express joy and gratitude. Grandpop was the most joyful man I've ever known, and I have often wondered how people are able to feel this way consistently.

"And whatever you do, in word or deed, do everything in the name of the Lord Jesus, giving thanks to God the Father through him."[97]

---

[97] English Standard Version (ESV), Colossians 3:17

Since I'm naturally caring and appreciative of people for being "themselves," I've always maintained dubious concerns about everything and everyone because we are going to get hurt if we leave the door open for everyone – right? Throughout my writings in this journal I've expressed that openness is a requirement for *meek strength*. Being "opened up" for God's intervention in our lives is where *meek strength* is the most powerful and significant. However, this openness also exposes us to various expressions that have corruptible influences in the *material* world, which God allows.

When we faithfully believe it, the Power of Prayer becomes a natural defense offering a "screen door" that allows the fresh air and sunshine of His Purpose in and forbids large obstructions to disrupt momentum. Our imperfections along the *path* will humble us on the journey at times, but as long as we are open to the Spirit, we will be confident in His Purpose.

"For you bless the righteous, O Lord; you cover him with favor as with a shield." [98]

Just as a meek horse was trained to endure the intense commotion, distress, and uncertainty of battle and will not budge without a command from his master, we must observe a similar *spiritual* alignment with our Heavenly Master, which is already programmed within us. Although the war horse and rider are individual warriors separately, when they are joined together for a specific purpose in battle they become one complete weapon. As four eyes detect imminent danger with precise focus at a blurring pace, and three ears listen to the roaring sounds of destruction there is one ear attuned only to the voice of the master. When our Master's Voice whispers to us we perceive direction no matter how loud the external environment is; as long as we are open to the command.

Joy will never be found without openness, as the walls formed around ourselves seal in toxins and shelter us from our greatest source

[98] English Standard Version (ESV), Psalm 5:12

of power on earth – sunshine and Truth. When we find it difficult to share happiness with others, our door is closed. When situations and circumstances are all about us, our door is closed. When we lack compassion and understanding, our door is closed to Almighty God as He offers both to us through the Spirit. Being closed to God is "death" in this life contrary to popular belief. We are eternal *spirit* beings so how relevant is it that our "death" would be entirely applicable to life after death?

"For God so loved the world, that he gave his only begotten Son, that whosoever believeth in him should not perish, but have everlasting life." (John 3:16, KJV).

Prayer is our shield against fear and doubt, which are barriers to openness. Why should we consistently harbor fear or doubt when we are covered by the Most High? We are the results of what we believe and our beliefs exist all around us in our *material* reality whether we acknowledge them or not. Are we believing to start a company and we haven't taken one business course or had an in-depth talk with a business owner? In this example, we are only thinking about starting a company. Are we believing for a right time to enroll in a training program or return to college but don't have a timeframe or curriculum plan because we don't have money or time to develop a plan? In this example, we may want to seek training or go to college but it probably won't happen. A true belief requires that we have both a *spiritual* premise and a *material* way forward.

"14 What does it profit, my brethren, if someone says he has faith but does not have works? Can faith save him? 15 If a brother or sister is naked and destitute of daily food, 16 and one of you says to them, "Depart in peace, be warmed and filled," but you do not give them the things which are needed for the body, what does it profit? 17 Thus also faith by itself, if it does not have works, is dead." (James 2:14-17; NKJV)[99]

When we decide to follow our true dream we are in fact led by the Spirit to the *edge of the beginning of our journey toward our inheritance*. With *meek strength* we pray for guidance as we step on the golden path toward our legacy. Following that "inner" voice of truth, humbly seeking continuous guidance from God, and expecting the manifestation of God's Promise by faith exemplifies how we glorify the Father. Together and individually we are the *material* body of Jesus Christ on earth and in the "flesh" to do the miraculous works that Jesus was able to do. As it is written, we can also expect even "greater works" from the Father — if we believe. Is that what He said in John 14:12? I believe so! Faith is exhibited through action, radiated by our bodies, and maximized with constant prayer. Sounds like faith is a verb that "underlines" everything we do and we must pray to carry it out with a powerful effect.

Bottom line: constant prayer maximizes faith by consciously lifting the focus of achievement off our limited human potential to enhance confidence, commitment, and appreciation in God's Plan for our lives.

"If I alone bear witness about myself, my testimony is not true."
– John 5:31

PART SEVEN
The End of Self

I once conducted a six-month long "*self*" experiment when I was 19 years old to deny my-*self* certain interests that I considered to be typical activities of the young adult kind. Some of these "infamous" male preoccupations included drinking alcohol, sex, cursing, bar hopping, and eating red meat – yes, red meat. At this time, I was enlisted in the U.S. Army and stationed in Germany where all of those activities were "legal" for my age. In my spare time though, I was reading books written by Henry David Thoreau, Ralph Waldo Emerson, Martin Luther King, Mahatma Gandhi and others, whose philosophical and social values intrigued me.

These bold men had adopted values that were counterintuitive to what many of us believe in society and therefore, they were revolutionary in thought and practice. As far back as I could remember, I was sensitive to the hardships of people and knew to some extent that individuals were responsible for the issues that showed up in their lives. I wanted to see what it felt like to give up the normal human daily pursuits that often distracted young men like me from self-awareness. I wanted to be "perfect" in some-thing and now was my time to find out what that something was with few distractions. The problem with my perspective at that time was that I presumed that perfection was an appropriate and attainable goal. It is not.

Throughout our Christian history and faith traditions there has been only one perfect human being mentioned, and his name was Jesus Christ. Our purpose for being here, as spirit in *material* flesh is not to be perfect, but to re-discover who we are and to *journey toward our inheritance*. I believe a practice in perfectionism is a mythical attempt. The path can become long, difficult and hopeless when we begin a mythical journey. Seeking perfection and striving to do our best are two different ideals. Aspiring to be perfect is driven by ego and the desires of the *material* self.

When we are "real" with ourselves and our practices we understand that perfection is unattainable in our human bodies. As the 18th century poet Alexander Pope revealed, "to err is human."[100] We are flawed by human nature in order to experience our-*selves*, and realize that without God we are empty *material* beings. When we reach that degree of wisdom, we are "fearfully" inspired to acknowledge His presence in our lives to fulfill our true purpose. It is not possible to experience our true potential without acknowledging God.

My six-month "empirical" study of *self*, while stationed in Germany was enlightening to say the least. I won the "conscious" battles with ego but I was powerless against my subconscious mind that overwhelmed me with my own desires while dreaming during sleep. That was an outcome I was not prepared for. The *self* wants what it wants based on a mixture of internal biochemical factors and external influences. However, I'm learning to balance this outlook by paying close attention to both my conscious and subconscious thoughts.

Through prayer we ask for counsel and correct judgment on the *path,* and through meditation we listen to what our subconscious mind is saying when we shut off all external influences. There are "silent scripts" of the subconscious mind running programs in the background of our mind 24-hours a day. If we aren't consciously writing these scripts with favorable thoughts and emotions, our subconscious mind is creating them for us – good and bad! When we neglect our

---

[100] BrainyQuote, Alexander Pope http://www.brainyquote.com/quotes/authors/a/alexander_pope.html

subconscious thoughts they punish us with nagging allusions of failed and incomplete attempts that flavor our emotions with feelings of guilt and doubt.

Our ancient ancestors have known for thousands of years that we have two minds: a masculine conscious mind and a feminine subconscious mind; and guess which one is more powerful. The conscious mind creates without a set timeframe about 5% of the time bouncing here and there according to our physical experiences. Where the conscious mind isn't focused on creating in our present reality, the subconscious mind takes over through habits and learned behaviors. According to Dr. Bruce Lipton, a bio-scientist in Epigenetics, the subconscious mind runs 95% of our lives and is a million times more powerful than the conscious mind! Furthermore, our "mind, absolutely, controls our biology, behavior and genetics." [101]

For example, if an organism perceives its environment to be hostile, the brain will release chemicals into the body to produce a "biology" to deal with those threats. Conversely, if an organism perceives an environment to be loving, the brain will release the appropriate chemistry to manifest experiences that relate to it. Dr. Lipton explains in "Conscious vs. the subconscious thinking" (YouTube) that Epigenetics is the science of how an organism perceives its environment and "selects" the complementary genetics in order to conform to it effectively. [102]

Wow! We are capable of selecting and modifying our genes to correspond to our *material* world whether we are aware of these selections and modifications – or not. Think about this for a minute: the subconscious mind creates our lives 95% of the time from the learned programs we've downloaded from our families and the personal habits we've developed over time. To observe how our subconscious mind has either helped or hindered our lives, we need to "mindfully" understand the current circumstances of our lives.

Our lives today are primarily a reflection of our subconscious

---

[101] YouTube Conscious vs. the subconscious thinking http://www.youtube.com/watch?v=M1kW0bHtY38

[102] Ibid.

thoughts. Is your current life the one that you would consciously create again? If we would not choose our current lives again, we should turn our attention to being more self-conscious. In this context, self-consciousness relates to being present and aware of the choices we make, while in the moment through self-reflection. If we are aware of the choices and how we feel making them as they arise, we are able to evaluate both the decisions and results. Self-awareness drives effective creation as we do not revert to stale habits and lifestyle behaviors, which is creation by default.

I am an avid daydreamer and while I'm "dream-walking" to familiar destinations, I've often wondered how I arrived there when I didn't remember passing certain places or making specific turns. I learned from Dr. Lipton that when our conscious mind wanders to focus on other issues and divides attention between two tasks, the subconscious mind habitually takes over one of those tasks. Multi-tasking is a trick the subconscious mind plays on us since we can only assume tasks consciously one at a time. All the other things we think we are doing at the same time are driven by our subconscious mind according to learned behaviors.

The powerful subconscious mind is committed to replaying a specific scenario over and over again, until it "magically" appears to be real. However these processes aren't magical; they are routine and predictable. As we create a vision in our wandering conscious mind, the subconscious mind "underwrites" the tasks left to it according to routine programming. In the previous example of dream-walking, as I'm considering how to get more business clients and additional funding to expand my commercial reach, my subconscious mind is leading me without my awareness or input. Scary, huh?

Even though it takes us a while to realize that we are "wonderfully made" to accomplish everything God has for us, it's still hard to understand how the conscious and subconscious mind work for our good. In accordance with the duality principles of the Principle of Polarity, the masculine conscious mind and feminine subconscious mind "procreate" in harmonic passion to yield the manifestation of our dreams into our *material* reality.[103]

The "technology" of our bodies and the "programs" that run in us require an active balance of a masculine and feminine dual aspect. When we do this right our masculine conscious mind uses its 5% of influence to plant the *seed* of a focused idea into the fertile *soil* of the feminine subconscious mind. This could be five minutes that makes a dream come true! Fertile soil relates to a healthy subconscious mind that has been cultivated by self-awareness, treated with recurring affirmative thoughts of our intention, and nourished with good feelings expressed by joy and gratitude.

As I understand it, when our subconscious mind is balanced appropriately, it commits a higher share of that 95% mentioned earlier to producing the focused idea of the conscious mind into our *material* reality. This is "free will" that drives our lifestyles and abilities to be led by the Spirit *on the journey toward our inheritance.* We must choose to be self-aware of intentions and feelings in order to manifest the Goodness of God.

Under the Divine Providence of God it takes dual aspects of our lives to fully experience our *material* reality. Additionally, Gregg Braden, a well-known scientist and author seeks to bridge science and spirituality through ancient wisdom. He speaks, eloquently, on how our individual bodies impact our *material* existence. He stated during a YouTube seminar about *The Divine Matrix* that "the union of human thought and emotion creates a feeling of belief and this feeling is a language" in itself.[104]

Our feelings tell our bodies and our surroundings what we are really thinking. If you don't believe it, take a quick look around your personal spaces at home and work and evaluate your initial feelings for about a minute. The feedback or feeling we receive from those environments is only a reflection of our initial thought output. In other words, our thoughts and emotions either consciously or subconsciously spoke to those places what we wanted to see in them right now.

---

[103] *The Kybalion*, by Three Initiates, (1912), http://www.sacred-texts.com/eso/kyb/kyb04.htm

[104] Gregg Braden, *The Divine Matrix:* http://www.bing.com/video/search?q=Gregg+Braden%2c+The+Divine+Matrix&qpvt=Gregg+Braden%2cThe+Divine+Matrix&FORM=VDRE

Our masculine thoughts and feminine emotions "married" to produce a feeling, which brought about a specific condition in our bodies to influence the external environment we exist in at this very moment. There are no accidents or coincidences; there is only conscious and subconscious idea manifestation – creation.

Braden has travelled the world and spoken to peoples of various cultures who still live according to the ancient wisdom and practices of old. He reminds us that societies outside of the Western world have known these truths for thousands of years, but we have somehow forgotten them.

Hold on tight for this next statement. There is scientific research and evidence that our emotions change the DNA in our bodies, and this DNA physically changes the matter around us.[105] The strands of our DNA are longer when we are relaxed and tighten and shorten when we are stressed. When our hearts express feelings of gratitude and appreciation we effect our DNA strands and environment in positive ways.

Our hearts are the most powerful electrical and magnetic instrument in our bodies.[106] This remarkable "technology" has a measurable radius of influence for individuals, and its massive power can be identified from space via satellite pictures of earth, while groups of people are worshipping.

The story of our human biological evolution is the smaller story among a more prominent History. The organic composites of our bodies integrated in a "Matrix" with both a *spiritual* and *material* "fabric" is a design that could have only resulted from a mighty Divine Creator. This Matrix or Mind of God allows us to create our world based on the faith of our beliefs.

When we believe that our sicknesses are already healed, our businesses are already flourishing, and our soul mates are already in our lives, we have already achieved close to 100% of the victory. But the smaller percentage of our victory left to patience is often intimidated

---

[105] Dr. Bruce Lipton, The Biology of Belief (1991, 2004)

[106] Gregg Braden, *The Divine Matrix:* http://www.bing.com/videos/search?q=Gregg+Braden%2c+The+Divine+Matrix&qpvt=Gregg+Braden%2c+The+Divine+Matrix&FORM=VDRE

by subconscious visits from fear and doubt that weaken the faith of our stated beliefs. Remember – our belief system changes the perspectives associated with the *material* of our reality. Sometimes this can happen immediately.

During the Braden YouTube video about *The Divine Matrix*, he presents a video showing a lady with a malignant tumor in her bladder being treated in China with energy faith healers.[107] The faith healers perform a vibratory chant translated to mean "already done" and the tumor shrinks out of sight in two minutes and forty seconds! The healers' focused energy vibrations on the tumor in harmony with the patient's inner focused belief resulted in an immediate recovery without any physical intervention. I believe here we are reminded that:

"A man's belly shall be satisfied with the fruit of his mouth; and with the increase of his lips shall he be filled. Death and life are in the power of the tongue: and they that love it shall eat the fruit thereof." (Proverbs 18:20-21, KJV)

I remembered my grandfather praising God for many years after delivering him from bladder tumors, while in his 70s. He wouldn't allow doctors to perform surgery because he was faithful there would be a spiritual resolution. He truly believed he was iron testimony for the Goodness of God and wouldn't accept any other viewpoint.

Grandpop lived to the age of 93, but was really sick in his final month because his physical body was ailing, and he refused to rest. Although he lives in eternity now, I believe he would still be with us if he could have exchanged his worn out "vehicle" for an updated model before transcending to the Infinite Source of Life. He had an uncommon love of life.

These faith examples should be of no surprise to those of us who have spent many years in a *spiritual* practice. However, for me it still is. I get "goose bumps" when I witness miracles even though we should have a standard expectation for these wonders. We should humbly expect to be blessed and healed under any condition, as we

---

[107] Ibid.

94

are equipped with both the physical and *spiritual* "technologies" to manifest our intentions.

"Jesus replied, 'I tell you the truth, if you have faith and do not doubt, not only can you do what was done to the fig tree, but also you can say to this mountain, 'Go, throw yourself into the sea,' and it will be done.'" (Matthew 21:21, NIV)[108]

We all have a "mountain" or large unwanted circumstance to cast into the sea, and some of us have more than one. In Jesus' reply, He cautions us to have faith and not doubt to fulfill our intent. Since the conscious mind is always occupied with our present circumstances, fear and doubt are perpetually in the background playing "hooky" from legitimate concerns and making a big deal out of irrelevant issues. They constantly pervade our subconscious mind by repeating whispers of failed attempts and worries that dilute our confidence.

To have the faith to move mountains, we should saturate fear and doubt with *A Psalm of David* (Psalms 23), by repeating the "song" out loud with certainty. Fear and doubt are in the same energy field as courage and confidence and repeating Psalms 23 often will offer the subconscious mind a recording that plays to our advantage. Try it.

Fear and doubt are only "shadows" of potential risks and are harmless since a risk is not yet a *material* substance. When we are consciously aware of potential threats we can evaluate and accept legitimate concerns to soften their effects and measure the credibility of others. Maintaining high levels of stress from the symptoms of fear and doubt cause our bodies to produce biochemicals (cortisol) to deal with perceived threats. Under these conditions, our bodies are programmed to convert proteins to sugar for an energetic "fight or flight" response.

However, with no *material* dangers to deal with, increased cortisol production will manifest symptoms of depression, anxiety, nervousness, irritability, and high blood pressure, according to WebMD.[109] Furthermore, we carry the physical symptoms of fear and

---

[108] New International Version (NIV), Matthew 21:21

[109] What Is Cortisol? https://www.webmd.com/a-to-z-guides/what-is-cortisol#1

doubt around with us as a negative energy field that may attract disease or death. One of the most famous speeches about fear was offered by Franklin D. Roosevelt during his First Inaugural Address in 1933: "This great Nation will endure as it has endured, will revive and will prosper. So, first of all, let me assert my firm belief that the only thing we have to fear is fear itself..."[110]

He spoke to citizens about the "dark realities of the moment" and the common difficulties shared among everyone. What is remarkable about this presentation was the tremendous courage he had to deliver a message like this one.

He reminded a nation that even in those depressed economic times there were no locust swarms and dangers comparable to what the forefathers had encountered. The collective issues and concerns, according to FDR involved "material things" and wealth. There had been no failure of material "substance" that resulted in the economic depression, but a failure of practice and process by the "rulers of the exchange of mankind's goods," and "unscrupulous money changers." Do any of these issues sound familiar and have legitimacy today?

Fear and doubt are immaterial – of no matter or substance. However, there are *material* root causes for these shadow appearances and the louder the voices of fear and doubt are the deeper we must dig to uncover their real sources. For example, I have realized through the results of "hard won" challenges that a source of fear for me was having differing viewpoints and representing them in assembled gatherings.

Since I was a young child I was aware that I was a bit different from my peers but I liked it then because my "uniqueness" wasn't interpreted as a challenge to others. Many people accepted and loved it, and in response I loved them. But as an adult I've noticed that personal differences can be perceived as an affront to the normal balance of order.

I sought refuge in my early life through readings of the famous society outsiders throughout history mentioned earlier. I was content to be different, as I thought this was the way God made me. Ralph

---

[110] "Only Thing We Have to Fear Is Fear Itself": FDR's First Inaugural Address, http://historymatters.gmu.edu/d/5057/

Waldo Emerson had written, "whoso would be a man, must be a nonconformist" in *Self Reliance and Other Essays*.[111] My ego wore it as a badge of courage until...it didn't work for me anymore. In just about every meeting, classroom, conference, assembly, or other gathering, I've always found myself to be alone in thought, perspective, and feeling. Over time in my work environments this led to feelings of anxiety and doubt in my ability to present ideas I believed to be solutions for ordinary issues.

I had grown tired of repeatedly facing the same difficulties in people-driven environments with the same answers because of arrogance and indecision. Additionally, in staff meetings at work it did not help circumstances or my own perceptions when the merits of my responses were met with opposition in favor of "typical" proposals. It took me about five years of conscious self-reflection to finally admit to my-*self* that I was different, and I was chasing dreams that weren't mine. However, it only took one day to accept that reality.

When anxiety began yelling at me, I promptly joined a Toastmasters International Club and began work on enhancing my improvisation, presentation, and other oral communication skills. In corporations and government agencies alike many leaders are required to speak to large and small audiences to influence social, public, and policy debates. The website About Us page states that Toastmasters International "is a non-profit educational organization that teaches public speaking and leadership skills through a worldwide network of meeting locations."[112]

Toastmasters prepares individuals for addressing all audiences by helping us accept our own unique voice to master specific techniques of speaking. The meetings offer unique oral drills to encourage and evaluate confidence in speaking among others who desire to improve the same skills. The meetings are so fun and interactive that you don't even realize you're building a sound foundation in verbal communication.

---

[111] Good Reads, *Self Reliance and Other Essays* Quotes http://www.goodreads.com/work/quotes/1472936-self-reliance-and-other-essays-dover-thrift-editions

[112] Toastmasters International Website http://www.toastmasters.org/members/membersfunctionalcategories/aboutti.aspx

After only one year, I volunteered to compete in Toastmasters contests with other club members throughout the region who had competed for many years. I didn't win but I felt wonderful because my club peers and the club president encouraged me to do it. In the first year I developed a fondness for my ability to deliver an unwritten speech in a distinctive manner – my voice.

I no longer encountered the same overwhelming anxiety and doubt when delivering my ideas and perspectives. Now I expect that my responses will be different and when others don't agree, it's okay. My ego is resolved today and one discussion at a time.

"Thus also faith by itself, if it does not have works, is dead," (James 2:17, NKJV).[113]

The ancient Greek philosopher, Socrates, is presented in plays written by Plato to have dedicated his life to learning, ethics, and questioning the observations in our *material* lives. In the years between 470-399 BC and over 2,400 years ago, Socrates was endowed with a wisdom, a knowledge and an understanding he knew could only be a reflection of God's Mind.

Socrates wouldn't even accept that he was the wisest man alive at the time, even though everyone else was willing to give him that title. He understood that by accepting the title of wise was in fact, making him unwise. Socrates explains this in the following excerpt of a speech entitled *The Apology*: "...but the truth is, O men of Athens, that God only is wise; and by his answer he intends to show that the wisdom of men is worth little or nothing;..."[114]

Socrates' response to being the "wisest" man was, "I know that I know nothing."[115] This adherence to meekness underscores the primary objective for me writing this journal after bumping into my own ego imperfections. We must be humble enough to accept that we are empty vessels without God's Promise. Socrates would pose questions for men

---

[113] New King James Version (NKJV), James 2:17

[114] Encyclopedia Britannica, Plato's Apology: https://www.britannica.com/biography/Socrates/Platos-Apology

[115] Ibid.

and society to explore their own truths of understanding without offering an answer. He knew that when he presented a question to the "wisest men" he could find at the time, they would answer with the inadequate knowledge inherent in their own human perceptions.

With this limited understanding, they would reveal themselves to be unwise. More importantly he maintained that our belief and practice be simultaneous in our lives as we are happier beings on a quest for *self*-improvement. I'm even more encouraged on my journey now after realizing that we are not required to have all the answers about our lives, but we are obliged to explore and learn our-*selves*.

By 2012, I was fed up with my-*self* and although I had not hit "rock bottom" yet, I was as far gone as I could tolerate. I was working part-time without success to attract clients and investors for my company and rousing adversaries at my full-time job. When I wasn't working or involved in family activities, I was at "happy hour" drinking cocktails in large quantities to "take the edge off" of life, as I've heard other people say. I could feel that I needed to modify my behavior, and my wife tried to convince me to make a change, but sometimes ego can be more convincing.

While working as a member of the senior management team for over two years, the director of the agency announced her retirement. I had initially applied for a position at this agency because of the reputation it had for employee recognition and advocacy programs. I felt an overwhelming sense of doom and gloom during her retirement party on Friday, June 1, 2012 and for a good reason. After leaving another party that night, I was arrested for driving under the influence (DUI) at 1am on June 2nd.

I discovered immediately on June 2nd that ego tells us who we think we are, and our actions tell us who we really are. The arrest introduced me to who I was at that time: arrogant, irresponsible, and selfish. With my head in my hands and feeling down and out, I made a promise to my-*self* while sitting in the jail cell. It wasn't a vow of perfection this time but a vow of *self*-improvement that included giving up drinking alcohol for two years. I didn't know how I was going to recover from this incident, but I knew it was going to be a long, difficult and embarrassing march uphill. And, if I was going to do it wisely, I needed to do the opposite of what I would normally do under the circumstances.

As I've stated often, when we are open to change the Spirit leads us to the sources of discovery to find more pieces of our mystery puzzle. However, "you can lead a horse to water but you can't make it drink."[116] I was ready this time to take the necessary steps for dramatic change but in hindsight, I'm not sure I would have been as eager without an extreme wakeup call. Even when we aren't willing to accept our *anointing*, we are never able to outrun it. It continues to follow us until one or more life perceptions stir up enough inspiration for us to recognize it.

My goal-driven ego valued achievement above all, and my road to humility began in recognizing the strengths of others and the weaknesses in my-*self*. According to Plato, "know thyself" was a central teaching of Socrates but what does this truism really mean? You may have heard this ancient saying before and may even have an understanding of how it could relate to your life. But I offer you an additional perspective, which allows me to be completely satisfied on my current *path*.

The only reason you are here at this time on earth is to understand who you are and to re-member and assemble the pieces of the puzzle together for your truth. When you begin to take seemingly random pieces out of the metaphorical box and put them together, a portion of a "picture" will appear that you may have overlooked before.

From obscure to obvious, the picture recognition arrives suddenly as an epiphany or experience we know to be true. It causes us to feel alive and excited, but if you've never felt the sensation before it can also be felt as a sudden rush of confusion. Either way the feeling is analogous to an awakening that shakes the mind and soul and culminates in the body as a blissful sensation – joy!

This abrupt sensation happened to me while reading Paul Coelho's novel, *The Alchemist*. After we experience an awakening of the soul, we are unable to return to the slumber of ignorance. We must

---

[116] The Phrase Finder: *Old English Homilies* http://www.phrases.org.uk/meanings/you-can-lead-a-horse-to-water.html

proceed with identifying other pieces of our mystery puzzle, and the Spirit will lead us right to the *edge of the beginning of our journey.*

Coelho, in *The Alchemist* presents a beautiful narrative about a young shepherd who leaves a small quiet Spanish town in search of his "personal legend," which is the dream that represented his greatest desire. We all have one, and the book clearly illustrates that it fades away gradually as we age. *The Alchemist* opened the first door to my soul when Melchizedek mentioned to Santiago that we all buy into "the world's greatest lie."[117] The world's greatest lie, he says is "that at a certain point in our lives, we lose control of what's happening to us, and our lives become controlled by fate."[118] I not only bought that lie, I financed and mortgaged it!

The author offers a specific process for getting us started on our journey and I used this method as I began the walk on my *path.* The process I'm referring to is a tithe or faith-offering of one-tenth of earnings to a church, charity, foundation or other cause. Tithing demonstrates our commitment to believing that God will provide everything we need at just the right moment.

This also relates to "sowing a seed" of faith in our own dreams by giving to others. I had never been a big advocate of tithing, as I gave what I felt like giving above and below the ten percent. But there are *spiritual* laws that support giving to others when we are "standing on the promises of God," as illustrated in the following scripture.

"One gives freely, yet grows all the richer; another withholds what he should give, and only suffers want. Whoever brings blessing will be enriched, and one who waters will himself be watered." (Proverbs 11:24-25, ESV)[119]

In the book the main character, Santiago, meets Melchizedek who mentions that he is the "King of Salem" and encourages him to continue pursuing his dream.[120] However, he asks Santiago for one-

---

[117] Paulo Coelho, *The Alchemist* (New York: HarperCollins, 1998), 18.

[118] Ibid.

[119] English Standard Version (ESV), Proverbs 11:24-25

[120] New American Standard Bible (NASB), John 16:7-9

tenth of his sheep and then he would help him. This part of the book opened a second door to my soul, as prior to this reading I had been "bombarded" with sermons and teachings on tithing that I consciously ignored. My father even mentioned it during a miscellaneous discussion in reference to paying bills.

But when I rediscovered this overlooked piece of my mystery puzzle in a place where I wasn't expecting it, I knew I had to do it. Now I understand what it means to be convicted by the Spirit.

"7 But I tell you the truth, it is to your advantage that I go away; for if I do not go away, the Helper will not come to you; but if I go, I will send Him to you. 8 And He, when He comes, will convict the world concerning sin and righteousness and judgment; 9 concerning sin, because they do not believe in Me." (John 16:7-9, NASB)[121]

Prior to resigning my position to work full-time in my company, I gave two-thirds of the money I had saved in my business account to the church in Elkhorn where I grew up.

There were several reasons for choosing to "sow" two-thirds of the money I had saved for business at that time instead of the one-tenth, which is a smaller amount. It wasn't an enormous amount of money but one-tenth means one dollar out of 10, and two-thirds is equivalent to two dollars out of three. I challenged my-*self* and my faith by leaving my bank account almost empty but for good reasons I believed.

First, I wanted to observe how God would replenish my business account before the insufficient balance fees accumulated and the account closed. I wanted to increase the impact of giving and consciously observe good things manifesting in plain view. I also wanted to inform my community that I was starting a company to continue the "work" of my grandfather in a similar manner that seemed to be true for me as well.

My business account has been replenished many times in cycles through my 401k liquidation, client payments, and vending location

---

[121] New American Standard Version (NASB), John 16:7-9

sales, but I've seen my bank balances swing like a person swatting away gnats. The expression of faith isn't for the faint of heart. You've got to believe the unseen to know it will happen.

Many readers may also recall that Melchizedek is mentioned in the Old Testament of the Bible in Genesis as the "king of Salem and priest of God Most High." In Genesis 14:19-20 Melchizedek blessed Abraham and joined him in celebration of the defeat of kings.[122] During the meal of bread and wine, Abraham offered Melchizedek one-tenth of everything he had recovered from victory in battle. The blessing and subsequent offering of one-tenth of everything gained in conquest is representative of the relationship we should have with God after a victory and while we are believing for one.

I don't have words to describe the impact this novel has had on my life. I was previously aware of the book for years, but I only decided to read it when I was experiencing a downward spiral in my life and managing just enough hopelessness to be open to it. Please understand that a level of soul maturity is required to process the reading and truths that are mentioned throughout. As it is written in the Book of Hebrews 5:14:

"But solid food is for the mature, who by constant use have trained themselves to distinguish good from evil."[123]

Many truths are hidden from us in archaic languages, statues, and structures, and passed down to us in scriptures, proverbs, axioms, and clichés – some of which I included throughout this journal. Very often when we are confronted with truth it seems foreign and uncomfortable, because we are challenged by it. When something challenges our sensibilities and intellect we are typically offended by it, even when it's in our best interest. I've learned the more appropriate response is: "where did you find that information? I will check it out and get back with you."

The *self* must know humility and God, in order to blossom

---

[122] New International Version (NIV), Genesis 14:19-20
[123] New International Version (NIV), Hebrews 5:14

and witness the "fruits" of joy, patience, and faithfulness. The signs, indicators, and warnings of our-*self* surround us at this very moment, and the people closest to us can see them too. When we are open and aware of the imbalances in our lives, the first step to the *edge of the golden path* is to acknowledge the changes we want to see, and ask God for help. With sincerity, we have just opened up a broad lifeline to the Most High, and He will send counsel of the Spirit. However, the answer we receive isn't always the one we expect, but whatever God has for us is the *path* to meaning, joy and purpose we won't find on our own.

If you want to be, financially, rich and joyful, you must find faith in God first. If you want to be an entertainer, with a joyful promise, you must find faith in God first. If you want to be an exuberant entrepreneur – trust me, you must find faith in God first! Let my journey assure you that when you find out what God has for you first, nothing else is comparable.

"But seek first His kingdom and His righteousness, and all these things will be added to you. So do not worry about tomorrow; for tomorrow will care for itself. Each day has enough trouble of its own." (Matthew 6:33-34, NASB)[124]

We all have a unique purpose for being here on earth at this time and place. If we look closely and evaluate our-*selves* we will find at least one thing we can individually perform better than anyone else. Just like individual snowflakes are unique no matter how many there are, we have distinctive traits that make us precisely the right size, height, and personality to fulfill our purpose.

Consider Earvin "Magic" Johnson, who played in the NBA for the Los Angeles Lakers as a point guard for thirteen seasons at an enormous 6 feet, nine inches tall. I wonder how many coaches and people told him that he was too tall to play the guard position and tried to convince him to play other positions.

Most point guards at that time, in the 1980s averaged only about

---

[124] New American Standard Bible (NASB), Matthew 6:33-34

6 feet in height, which has made Johnson a celebrated enigma. He was so gifted with size, vision, and ball handling theatrics that he could disarm opponents, while playing any position on the floor. But at the point guard position, his height offered a clear advantage for perceiving open players on the floor to deliver passes, with a rare consistency and style that created "Showtime" magic. When we are confident in, committed to, and appreciative of our true purpose in this life, it is expressed as brilliance.

I'm a natural visual artist but I don't like to draw or paint pictures. My father recognized my artistic interests around age 10 and enrolled me in art school, but I hated being taught how to do art. Art to me was a limitless expression of individual freedom that evolved at each moment toward completion. I didn't buy into learning the structure of contour lines and artistic elements, because it was boring to me.

As a result, I'm not a very good visual artist. I would rather sketch ideas, poems, proposals, plans, diagrams and technical manuals from scratch. I've found that all of these abilities originated from one muscular talent, which happens to be a creative mind. Since God offered me this manuscript, and I accepted on August 10th, 2013, I've been amazed by the content that just flows from a fellowship between the One Mind and my fingertips. We must submit to God's Will and align our talents with purpose to make life meaningful for us.

There are valid reasons why we believe we want to follow a specific *path* before submitting to God's Will for our lives. We may be following a dream because of what other people think about us, how we feel about ourselves, or we believe it will lead us to success and happiness. For sure I've had all of those feelings and beliefs at one time or another and even fulfilled my short-term goals with relative ease. Yet, I didn't feel successful or happy, which seems to coincide with other people, who are following everyone else's vision but their own.

Meek strength exists, so we don't need to worry about resources, success, or fortune and are able to advance toward our true vision with confidence, commitment, and appreciation. Many of the people in our lives won't agree with our true vision, and this may happen, because only we can see the actual "blueprint" of our dream inside our *selves*. For others to perceive our truth, in the beginning, they must be open to the same Spirit that is *leading us to the edge of our journey.*

Truth is eternal but "unseen" in the *material* world, which makes it difficult to sensibly discuss it. However, we feel and observe the "fruits" of Truth that manifest for all to see as testimony of God's Power, including patience in the midst of chaos and joy in the presence of pain.

To bring your dream into our physical *material* reality, you should have at least one other person, who "agrees" and supports you. If you're prepared to learn the "creation languages" of our thoughts, emotions, and feelings that are expressed as faith, patience, joy, love, and gratitude, you will have the things you want – and much more!

[11] *"And we desire that each one of you show the same diligence so as to realize the full assurance of hope until the end,* [12] *so that you will not be sluggish, but imitators of those who through faith and patience inherit the promises. "* (Hebrews 6:11-12, NASB)[125]

Bottom line: the Spirit leads the ego of self, with the talents that were developed for a specific purpose to the place where we have a material advantage.

---

[125] New American Standard Version (NASB), Hebrews 6:11-12

"But when he, the Spirit of truth, comes, he will guide you into all truth. He will not speak on his own; he will speak only what he hears, and he will tell you what is yet to come,"– John 16:13

PART EIGHT
The Holy Spirit is a GPS

For most of my life, I've wanted to be an attorney. I haven't always been conscious of the fact that I've associated my personal identity, or my-*self*, with the occupations I chose, as a means to sustain a living. I chose the *path* to becoming an attorney, because I had close family members and mentors, who had maintained prestige, honor and a good living from practicing law – and the career seemed so valiant.

I felt there were so many careers law school prepared a person for, such as being a prosecutor, defense lawyer, corporate lawyer, government lawyer, litigator, contract lawyer, judge, and using the credentials in politics and business. I considered the legal career to be a "power profession," and wasn't aware of any other education that offered this type of versatility.

I pursued this *path* in the beginning with "passion," and conducted exhaustive research on getting into a good law school, identifying internships and clerkships, getting letters of recommendation, and writing a personal statement for the admission application. As a pastime, I even viewed online attorney biographies to create a vision for "who" I might become.

In the beginning, with serious dedication and my admission

homework done, my desire to continue down this *path* smoldered and burned out, before I could get into a law school. Additionally, I found it difficult to accept that I could establish a goal and not complete it, which instantly prompted feelings of guilt and doubt.

Eventually, I conceded the notion of being unable to complete this goal by contemplating in "3-D" that the law profession was not my anointed *path*. The first observation occurred when I worked with numerous attorneys in my government career, and I discovered that many of them didn't like the work they were doing. Some, even felt trapped in their profession, since they had enormous student loan debt, were making a good salary and had grown accustomed to the lawyer prestige I was seeking. I began to question this career pursuit, as I struggled to find attorneys with personalities like mine, who enjoyed their law career.

Previously, in *Part Six*, I spoke of a top agency official, who offered me a "real" piece of advice that I refused to acknowledge, immediately, but I later appreciated. This was the second observation that informed me.

After taking the Law School Admission Test (LSAT) twice, and still being dissatisfied with the test score, I applied to one law school leaving the acceptance of my application to "fate." Since I never, truly, believed in fate, I recognized my rejection letter, as a third reason to modify my plan.

In hindsight, being admitted to business school may have facilitated an easier walk toward starting Pannell Enterprises LLC. Looking back at these occurrences, I find it much easier to evaluate the feelings that inspired me to make certain decisions. I believe the Spirit was right there, at each intersection whispering directions in my ear.

It took me a while to recognize that when we take on the full persona of "what we do," we accept a limited version of our-*selves*. There are more layers to our human nature than our jobs could ever represent. There is, certainly, more to life than being the people we are at work in every aspect of our lives. Although being in the Washington, D.C. metro area, people might not even talk to you, unless you are dressed in a certain way and have an acceptable job title.

In the most powerful city in the world, it pays in more ways than one to have a great job and friends with comparable or even better jobs. But when we have a good job, good pay and benefits, great professional networks, pleasant bosses and good working hours, and discontent still finds a slightly open door, we figure at that moment there is more to life.

While wrapped in human flesh, our spirit needs a continuous "broadband" connection to God because it is enclosed in *material* where the laws of space and time are imposed on it. In physics, the space-time continuum is the four dimensional "fabric" we exist in that makes us vulnerable to gravity, distance, and expiration (death) in a finite world. Due to our limited human nature, we need the Infinite Power of God to complete the works we were sent here to do.

The *Ethernet* was developed to join computers together in a shared system to transmit data faster and more reliably over local area networks (LANS). This shared network system is standard in work places and exists in many homes. According to Wikipedia, Ethernet technologies were conceived from the understanding that light needed a "medium" to travel through the vacuum of space.[126] In *Part Four*, I introduced a ubiquitous electromagnetic substance called ether, which transmits our thoughts and emotions, as vibrations through space-time to create our *material* reality. Does the Ethernet concept ring any bells? Imagine trying to do a research paper, send documents, or communicate with other people without the Internet. The Internet has made access to information and communications easy, immediate and available, at any time in our *material* world. It should be clear by now that information system technologies originate from how the Mind of God functions.

But the Mind of God is *material* and *spiritual*, while the Internet and Ethernet technologies harness only the finite capabilities of our physical existence. The Mind of God established the "ether" as our shared network to communicate with God, individually, and to worship together in Unity. The Mind of God has also, established the

---

[126] Wikipedia, Ethernet http://en.wikipedia.org/wiki/Ethernet

broadband sensation of feeling that we use to communicate with the Spirit. The most powerful information and communication sensation available, for our human experience is feeling.

God conceived the *path*, people and the Power needed for these works before we were born, and all we need is the openness to be *led to the edge of the path* to take the step onward. The Spirit is always available and awaits our call.

"But the Helper, the Holy Spirit, whom the Father will send in my name, he will teach you all things and bring to your remembrance all that I have said to you, " (John 14:26, ESV).[127]

Life is a *mystery*. In doubtful times, I've, repeatedly, asked questions like, "why are we here now; why were we created; why is life so difficult; why do kids die in such horrific ways; why am I alive; what does God want from me?" and many more. No one else can address questions like these for us. Only the *path* can take us to the Truth and Promise that we were created for, and the journey to God's Purpose will bring wisdom, understanding, revelation and people closer together. On the *path,* we re-discover who we are as both *spiritual* and *material* beings. We relearn our transcendent nature, while in human form, in order to manifest God's Purpose for us on Earth.

When we are not on the *path* to our inheritance, we are on the *path* to some-place. When we are not worshipping God, we are worshipping some-thing. Worship is exhibited through feeling, which makes it almost impossible to define. But the results of worship are clearly visible with open eyes. Since we become what we mostly think about and pay attention to, it follows logically that we also worship in those same areas. I worshipped ambition and success, as an adult, because I, previously, believed God wanted me and everyone else to be "successful," if they worked hard. The legend of success is a myth. The path can become long, difficult and hopeless, when we begin a mythical journey.

The term success means, absolutely, nothing without a context

---

[127]English Standard Version (ESV), John 14:26

to fit it into. Since every person expresses success, differently, by His Design, God has created a life for each of us to explore to achieve the sustainable happiness, purpose and meaning that is true for us. Success doesn't enter the equation, since achievement will happen, as long as we follow the "script" that was written for us.

When we ask God for our truth in prayer, He tells the Spirit the information to convey to our-*selves*, which is not subject to the same space-time limitations as our *material* self. Our spirit is eternal and when we neglect it, we disregard the most powerful and magnificent part of our *self*.

"In him you also, when you heard the word of truth, the gospel of your salvation, and believed in him, were sealed with the promised Holy Spirit, who is the guarantee of our inheritance until we acquire possession of it, to the praise of his glory." (Ephesians 1:13-14, ESV)[128]

When we apply reason and logic to the work of the Spirit, we come up short because reason and logic are *material* applications for objectives in our physical lives.

The Spirit is recognized through a combination of thought and emotion, which offers a feeling. And guess what? Worship and faith are exhibited through a feeling. So let's reason this out in a way that is familiar to us in the *material* world. Let's use logic. When we worship God and are faithful to our beliefs, we feel the presence of joy, purpose, and meaning in our lives. This feeling inspires the Spirit to guide us on the *path to our inheritance,* and we become aware of His Presence because we feel Him. It is also written:

⁵ He who has prepared us for this very thing is God, who has given us the Spirit as a guarantee. ⁶ So we are always of good courage. We know that while we are at home in the body we are away from the Lord, ⁷ for we walk by faith, not by sight. ⁸ Yes, we are of good courage, and we would rather be away from the body and at home with the Lord. ⁹ So whether we are at home or away,

----
[128] English Standard Version (ESV), Ephesians 1:13-14

we make it our aim to please him. (2 Corinthians 5:5-9, ESV)[129]

For people who may have a belief in God but have not shown the faith required to express joy in the face of chaos, to observe meaningful efforts in small contributions, and to manifest their tallest dream, this *Part* of the journal is dedicated to you. Each *Part* of this journal is written to explore the areas of spirituality that confused me.

Reason and logic ruled my world because I could apply it to any situation, based on observable criteria, and everyone could "see" whether or not it was accurate. But when I observed how hard I was working and how far I still needed to go to achieve my dream, I realized my *material* logic and circumstances didn't add up.

The consummate broadcast of *spiritual* and *material* resonance is more powerful than logic and reason, by Purpose. Since the 17th century Age of Reason, our search for "enlightenment" discouraged further consideration of our *spiritual* nature. At that time, it was thought that science was going to emancipate us from the archaic views of tradition and faith. However, science has come full circle and unveiled the Mind of God, which is now visible with current technologies. Google it yourself! There is no denying the fact that we live inside "The Matrix" or Mind of God, and humanists like me can observe that reality.

"For all things were created in Him, the things in the heavens, and the things on the earth, the visible and the invisible, whether thrones or dominions or principalities or powers, all things were created through Him and for Him. And He is before all things, and by Him all things consist." (Colossians 1:16-17, NKJV)[130]

The "Technologies" of God are, dependably, realized through meekness and worship. When we are happy because we are alive and breathing, we are worshipping God. When the *pendulum of equilibrium* swings misfortune with piercing heartache in our *material* reality, and we thank God for the comfort we are waiting on, we are worshipping

---

129 English Standard Version (ESV), 2 Corinthians 5:5-9,
130 New King James Version (NKJV), Colossians 1:16-17,

Him. When we thank God every day that we are one day closer to our "soul mates," because our closets, garages, and hearts have room...and we are open to the dual risks of openness expressed as both love and sadness, then we are exhibiting faith and worshipping God.

While in this season, I've found openness to be the singular way for accessing God, consciously, and, subconsciously, to realize our calling – our tallest dream. Being open brings along with it the risk of someone not meeting our expectations, but people can distress us even when we're closed. The difference here is the brighter rebound potential that is, only, available to those with open consciousness, which maintains a continuous lifeline to the Most High. Although I've established Pannell Enterprises LLC on my *path*, I'm nowhere near completion.

My journey for 13 weeks has, prayerfully, taken me to the doorway of preparing a collection of my most memorable experiences with a valid perspective. Hopefully these perspectives demonstrate there are no accidents or coincidences in this life. God has accounted for everything we do or will do, and to discover this Truth, we must *walk on the path to our inheritance*. I'm reminded almost, daily, there would be no easy way for me to work in the frozen food industry I'm in now without the knowledge I absorbed, while working with my grandfather, in his country store.

It's as though my service and response capability is instinctive, but it is not... it was learned. While filling frozen food and ice cream vending machines, I already know that newer products are always placed in the rear due to shelf life cycles, cargo loads for final delivery stops are placed in the front of the trailer, and the safe temperatures for hauling cold foods. I didn't study these and other related practices, but I confirmed with industry partners to be sure.

God's Will is Perfect and, surprisingly, easy to accomplish after we align ourselves and commit to it, which apparently has been a well-kept "secret." Our true work is easy for the *self* to comprehend and perform once we know what it is. But identifying the *path* and aligning our-*self* to it requires a diligent practice of faith and persistence. The distinction I wish to make here, is the difference between working hard to sustain a living and working hard to discover our true *path*.

When we work hard to find the pieces of the mystery puzzle for our lives with faith and bold perceptions of meaning and purpose, the intensity of awareness and passion becomes invigorating instead of draining. To be clear, if we're going to work hard at something, we should opt into what God has for us, and allow the Spirit to lead us to the *edge of the beginning of our journey*. The perception of working hard changes, as we begin to interpret work on the *path,* to be, as necessary and normal as breathing.

I explained in *Part One* that God prepared the *path* and everything we would need for our journey before we were born. We are required to be open to the experience of greeting the Spirit and allowing Him to lead us to it. I'm not saying, nor do I believe that finding the *path* is easy. This is a part of the mystery of life that only we can unfold individually, which is confusing at times. I am saying that what we are supposed to do, in this life, we were built to do it with a combination of *material* life experiences and physical attributes to align with the *spiritual* Purpose assigned by God. When we meet the face of purpose, we rediscover that we knew him our entire lives and like me, we may be humbled by the reunion.

I believed I had discovered a unique understanding of the way the Spirit guides me in making decisions and choosing options. I thought, "HS is like a supernatural Global Positioning System (GPS) that I can access for directions of any kind." I've even been lost on the road on the way to appointments without a functional GPS and pulled over to meditate for five or ten minutes to refocus. Without oversimplifying what happens, I do recognize that a short break with quiet-time does calm the body and mind enough to accept clear options. One of which may be to, simply, ask someone for directions.

The Holy Spirit must have been just as helpful to others, as He is to me, because when I did a Google search, recently, on "Holy Spirit and GPS" over 1.6 million results showed up. As it says in Ecclesiastes 1:9, *there is nothing new under the sun,"* and no matter how original we think our idea is, it has already been expressed before.[131] GPS devices are based on our interactions with technologies already in place known as Consciousness. To learn more, read books authored by Gregg Braden and Bruce Lipton, as they offer remarkable support that we are individual expressions of God's Mind being led to create and manifest the reality we exist in.

How many times have we input an address into a GPS device to get directions, only, to disregard them because we knew of a shorter route. I was notorious for doing that because I didn't trust the box and the hundreds of satellites in outer space to direct me fast enough. Additionally, the risk of a "recalculation" occurring just before a right turn was enough for me to toss that box out of an open window. The Spirit is, always, right there during these times extending patience, and with an open heart, I reach out and grab tightly. "Take a deep breath in and hold, now exhale slowly," is what He tells me, as I disregard anxiety that fear brought with him, and doubt soon exits, after I inform him I'm already late.

The companions of our human *self* get a free ride with us, and we allow it because we're open, right? The companions I speak of are fear, frustration, doubt, impatience, and the car isn't full until anger shows up. Done deal! Our human *self* is expressed as ego, in these situations, and as long as ego is driving, we are living, dangerously.

The Spirit exists for situations like these, since God knew we would be, vigorously, pursued and challenged by circumstances. In my life, during various phases, I've shown an extreme commitment to my *spiritual* self and my *material* self but at separate and distinct moments. It's the material-spiritual balance that God calls on us to exhibit because by denying either, we are inadequate, to pursue our true purpose.

If we are expected to observe only our *spiritual* nature as humans, then we are limited in our *material* incarnation by ignoring half of our dual nature. It's more helpful if we balance our *spiritual* and *material* needs, and allow the Spirit to lead both. If God wanted us

---

[131] New International Version (NIV), Ecclesiastes 1:9

115

to be perfect, He would have probably left us in the Infinite Spiritual Reality. Unfortunately, if you work in a kitchen with a nice suit on, you're bound to get some grease on it.

I would be overlooking the normal realities of life, if I didn't acknowledge that at times we become overwhelmed by our human nature. Unfair circumstances and challenging times are sometimes unavoidable, but we don't need to spend a lifetime in misery. During my misguided search for perfection, as a young adult, I rediscovered I was human, and no matter how hard I try, I will always have a potential to fail. The question to be asked and answered is: "who are we going to call after we fail?" It's, certainly, not going to be a GPS device – no directions to look for in there.

The trials of life are certain, but the Spirit awaits us at every turn. Sometimes we need to find ways to trick ourselves into a specific feeling, especially, when our external circumstances aren't supporting it. I've discovered three ways to do this, and I present them to you here in "3-D." First, research has shown that a smile triggers healthy chemical reactions in our bodies, and when we smile as a courtesy to others, we offer that same feeling to them. So find a way to smile even when you don't feel like it, and trick your body into a treat.

Secondly, I've needed to learn to make immediate changes, even when I didn't know what the outcomes would be. All I knew was that I didn't like the situations, emotions, and conditions of life at difficult times, and so, I just made an opposite choice moving forward. When I realized God was absent in my conscious life, I went on a search to find Him.

After I observed, that working in my professional career was taking me on a journey to a slow and painful death, I planned to leave and exited my job. And after my DUI charge, I stopped drinking alcohol, completely, for two years. I've found that sometimes just making an opposite decision may be enough to change an attitude and a behavior, and it only takes a second to commit.

The following idea is, probably, one of the most underappreciated and powerful methods for immediately transforming our feelings. Adopt a personal theme song or soundtrack for our lives! I know it might sound crazy or "corny" but think about it, for just a moment. Music is one of the oldest expressions of human nature, and the "universe sings" too.

Our sun recently sang a solo in our solar system! "Musical sounds created by longitudinal vibrations within the Sun's atmosphere, have been recorded and accurately studied for the first time by researchers, shedding light on the Sun's magnetic atmosphere."[132]

Remember the soundtrack for *Rocky III*? If you saw the movie, you probably guessed it immediately. It was the "Eye of the Tiger" by Survivor. In the Army, while preparing for physical fitness tests, I would listen to the song and recall the Rocky workout sessions, when he was preparing to fight Clubber Lang (Mr. T.). The song would instill a kind of mental "frenzy" that would promote excessive endurance. Since I have been an extreme personality at times, over-the-top preparation was the norm for me.

During Operation Desert Shield, I rode with Bob Marley's "Buffalo Soldier" in my headphones. At that time, I perceived myself as a "warrior" in peak mental and physical condition and refused any perspective other than we were going home, safely. I felt God's imminent presence, while I was there, because I knew my family and community were praying for my return. I had my M16 "locked and loaded," as I drove with my platoon sergeant on the passenger side, in a large "deuce and a half" or two and half ton truck through the barren desert of Saudi Arabia, on our way to Kuwait City.

My theme song on the *path* now is one of the many hits performed by my favorite band, Earth, Wind & Fire, entitled "That's The Way Of The World." Ever since I was 18, I've taken music by EW&F with me every place I've lived. The harmonic exchange among the brass, string, and percussion instruments are powerful enough to elevate my mood at any time.

When riding with me friends would ask if I had music to play and before I could respond, they would blurt out "Earth, Wind & Fire,

---

[132] ScienceDaily, Scientists discover heavenly solar music, (June 22, 2010): https://www.sciencedaily.com/releases/2010/06/100621101420.htm

I already know." From the very first musical note or string, I instantly know an EW&F song is about to play. Although my mind floats to a space far away on rhythmic wonders I'm unable to explain, the song's lyrical expression brings those emotions full circle by reverberating on the frequency of my heart.

We all have at least one song that makes us feel this way, and I'm convinced without conclusive evidence that the song is related to our true purpose in some way. Specific songs resonate with or "speak" to our inner voice based on the substance of our thoughts, emotions, and something even deeper in the *material* of our body and soul. Adopting a theme song for our journey encourages faithfulness to our dream, as the song lifts our most cherished thoughts to the surface, for us to feel without effort.

Since I redirected the passion of my heart to the "socio-economic" mission of Pannell Enterprises LLC, I'm able to re-imagine the sensation that inspires me every time I listen to That's The Way Of The World. When I open the door to the Spirit, He travels with me and dances with the same enthusiasm I feel. Don't be alarmed to know that while we sing and dance, He moves according to how we feel because we are One with the Almighty. Following is an excerpt of the song that stirs the zeal of my heart, as I journey the rolling hills toward my inheritance.

"Hearts of fire creates love desire
Take you high and higher to the world you belong
Hearts of fire creates love desire
High and higher to your place on the throne

We've come together on this special day
To sing our message loud and clear
Looking back we've touched on sorrowful days
Future pass, they disappear

You will find peace of mind
If you look way down in your heart and soul
Don't hesitate cause the world seems cold
Stay young at heart cause you're never, never old at heart

That's the way of the world
Plant your flower and you grow a pearl
A child is born with a heart of gold
The way of the world makes his heart grow cold."[133]

With the requirement of a *material* and *spiritual* dual balance to fully experience our humanity on earth, I also have a spiritual song, or psalm to sing. The Biblical Psalms were written to be sung with musical instruments. Although I don't know how to sing *A Psalm of David*, I speak the words aloud anytime I need to express confidence and commitment to ideas.

[1] The LORD is my shepherd, I lack nothing. [2]He makes me lie down in green pastures, he leads me beside quiet waters, [3] he refreshes my soul. He guides me along the right paths for his name's sake. [4] Even though I walk through the darkest valley, I will fear no evil, for you are with me; your rod and your staff, they comfort me. [5] You prepare a table before me in the presence of my enemies. You anoint my head with oil; my cup overflows. [6] Surely your goodness and love will follow me all the days of my life, and I will dwell in the house of the LORD forever. (Psalms 23, NIV)[134]

Be certain that when we lose interest and passion for our original goals and dreams, they are not true for us. God preinstalled a vision and purpose inside us before birth that will never diminish. However, it may become cloudy over time, when we don't act on it. When we turn down the volume of our human *self* or ego, we are able to hear the inner voice that speaks to us with profound influence. Also, be aware that our true dream may not be what we had envisioned for our-*selves*. But God makes no mistakes, and the guarantee is the Spirit that speaks only truth to us, when we are open to it.

Bottom line: when we are open to our-selves we can hear the Promise of God, which is preserved within us as a guarantee, and exists in those same proportions all around us.

---

[133] Metro Lyrics, That's The Way Of The World Lyrics http://www.metrolyrics.com/thats-the-way-of-the-world-lyrics-earth-wind-fire.html

[134] New International Version (NIV), Psalms 23

"I tell you, use worldly wealth to gain friends for yourselves, so that when it is gone, you will be welcomed into eternal dwellings... If you have not been trustworthy in handling worldly wealth, who will trust you with true riches? And if you have not been trustworthy with someone else's property, who will give you property of your own?"
– Luke 16:9-12 (NIV)

PART NINE
Money is a Means to a New Beginning

According to Wikipedia, "money is any object or record that is generally accepted as payment for goods and services and repayment of debts in a given socio-economic context or country."[135] The Merriam-Webster Dictionary says that currency is "paper money in circulation."[136]

I notice that our society is, conspicuously, obsessed with money because I hear about it all day and everywhere I go. However, it's not the money that people are, truly, preoccupied with; it's the currency named the dollar that we clamor about. There are at least three problems with this issue, simply, because we are not, totally, conscience of what we are fixated on. Please allow me to dissect the money concern by presenting it in "3-D."

The History of Money presented by PBS/NOVA explains that

---

[135] Wikipedia http://en.wikipedia.org/wiki/Money

[136] Merriam-Webster Dictionary, Currency: http://www.merriam-webster.com/dictionary/currency

paper currency was first used by China in 806 AD for 500 years until it disappeared, but long before Europeans began using it.[137] Prior to paper, people bartered by exchanging goods and services. Money has included livestock, sea shells, metal coins, strips of leather, gifts and beads.[138] In 1900, the U.S. linked gold, a precious metal to the dollar and later ended the Gold Standard in 1971.[139]

So, from '71 to current year 2020 our currency and financial system have depended on the "faith and trust" of Americans and its trading partners. It's interesting to me that there is so much talk about the dollar being in trouble because of America's debts to its trading partners throughout the world. I suppose our partners aren't willing to "forgive our debts," as it says in the King James Version of *The Lord's Prayer*.

The first problem here is that our entire global financial system, which includes the dollar, is based on the "faith and trust" of people, exclusively. The dollar goes only, as far as someone is willing to accept it, and although I'm a fan of having dollars in my pocket, I believe we should direct and focus our attention on developing the "inner vision" to attract it. While in the Army and stationed in Germany in 1990, I could spend dollars in the local economy to buy food or catch a cab, relatively, easy even though the value of the dollar was declining then. Now I'm told it's best to pay for things in the local economy with the local currency.

Open eyes will see that paper "currency" has no intrinsic value at all. Although beautifully crafted, it is a specially made paper that serves as a form of money, and it takes the form of tiny bits of electronic data when it's exchanged online. However, we place way too much thought energy on this "means" for buying things instead of the plan for becoming "attractive" candidates for wealth. Many people believe that money creates more money, in the form of riches and wealth. That is a myth. The path can become long, difficult and hopeless when we begin a mythical journey.

---

[137] NOVA, The History of Money http://www.pbs.org/wgbh/nova/ancient/history-money.html
[138] Ibid.
[139] Ibid.

Robert Collier, a 20th century philosopher and author said, "all riches have their origin in mind. Wealth is in ideas - not money."[140] I believe that faith in money diminishes our focus on the intent of an idea when our mental energy is, disproportionately, fixed on the money we are trying to achieve. Faith in God and His Idea is the *pathway* to eternal wealth.

"So we fix our eyes not on what is seen, but on what is unseen, since what is seen is temporary, but what is unseen is eternal." (2 Corinthians 4:18, NIV)[141]

We are often misled to place all focus and attention on our *material* world. But the *material* world is a finite and limited version of our eternal and unseen transcendent nature, which surrounds us and exists in us. Ideas are eternal, as they exist with no beginning or end in the One True Mind.

"What has been will be again, what has been done will be done again; there is nothing new under the sun." (Ecclesiastes 1:9 NIV)[142]

Just because we have an idea or even implement it before any other person does not make it original. That perspective alone should be humbling. All ideas are God inspired, and if they manifest in a way that is not good, the idea has been corrupted through the process of expression. God is Good and this Truth can never be any other way.

Adam Smith, who is known as the "father of economics," published *An Inquiry into the Nature and Causes of the Wealth of Nations* in 1776. This voluminous classic, aka *The Wealth of Nations*, is still the social and moral foundation of our economic system today – some 237 years later (1776 to 2013). As a social commentator with entrepreneurial perspectives akin to both John Mackey (Co-Founder/CEO of Whole Foods) and Ben Cohen (Co-Founder of Ben & Jerry), I believe that 21st century businesses should "maximize profits" with a

---

[140] **Robert Collier** Quotes http://www.brainyquote.com/quotes/authors/r/robert_collier.html
141 New International Version (NIV), Corinthians 4:18
142 New International Version (NIV), Ecclesiastes 1:9

good value for consumers and the communities they exist in.

Large and small commercial businesses alike have, actively, contributed to valid perceptions of engaging in greedy and selfish pursuits cloaked as competition. In exchange for "voluntarily" participating in the capital economy by purchasing common products, consumers are treated as though we deserve to be exploited in housing, insurance, investment income, and retirement savings.

Additionally, employees' abiding receipt of inadequate salaries relative to inflation and insufficient health benefits were further rewarded through persistent layoffs and furloughs in the private and public sectors. Open eyes will see that our economy is highly leveraged and susceptible to periodic violent swings toward disruption. Unfortunately, this isn't new phenomena, since the economic *pendulum of equilibrium* has swung back and forth from prosperity to poverty for thousands of years.

The second problem with our excessive attention on money involves the approach that individuals and companies employ to generate profits at the expense of people and established society. Smith's celebrated philosophy of "rational self-interest and competition leading to economic prosperity" has been, repeatedly, overwritten by irrational greed and selfish behaviors that have led to catastrophic economies on a global scale, routinely.

I believe businesses should support the communities they prosper in by offering goods and services at, reasonably, competitive prices. For example, if the citizens surrounding a company aren't able to afford the products of the residential business there is a fundamental misalignment between consumer expectations and commercial practices. The cheap real-estate and tax incentives for businesses in residential communities combined with exorbitant price obstructions for the local populace, doesn't promote a rational self-interest. These practices support a limited degree of commercial potential.

Within the context of offering a good product, I believe "value" is just as important as the product itself. In other words, I don't like to sacrifice quality for lower prices, but I don't want to pay enormous prices for quality either. I've established an innovative business practice with exceptional customer and client services, in a manner that has a "traditional" feel. Our low product prices along with attentive customer services offer Pannell Enterprises LLC an unrivaled competitive advantage.

A third problem with the excessive attention placed on money is that more people have obtained financial wealth now than at any other time in the history of civilization. However, this financial success has not translated to an overall increase in the feelings of well-being, as a result. I believe part of the reason extends to actors who have devoted over 237 years to promoting and acting in their own "self-interest."

Self-interest is interest of and for the *self.* In order for the *self,* to offer a benefit that serves the public interest, we need to, truly, know our-*self* and our intent. How can we expect an individual merchant to conduct business for him-*self,* appropriately, when his moral compass points in the direction of more currency at any cost? When our business practices aren't even good for our-*selves* with a *material* and *spiritual* balance, they will never be sufficient for any public good. I believe the intent of our *self*-interest is an abundant factor for determining how good we will serve the public interest.

Over 200 years of, obsessively, chasing money has deprived our world of a meaningful *material* and *spiritual* balance. The *material* world is to be governed by the individual expressions of God – us. God intended us to use His Power and not our *self*-interest only. Money is a "utility" to accomplish our true purpose, as an extension of the Creator and not "a means to an end." There is no end, because we are eternal spirit beings wrapped in perishable *material* "robes." Our spirit nature is much more significant to our lives, as we are only in *material* form to accomplish His Will.

"Do not love the world or the things in the world. If anyone loves the world, the love of the Father is not in him. For all that is in the world—the desires of the flesh and the desires of the eyes and pride in possessions—is not from the Father but is from the world. And the world is passing away along with its desires, but whoever does the will of God abides forever." (1 John 2:15-17, ESV)[143]

---

[143] English Standard Version (ESV), 1 John 2:15-17,

When the Will of God becomes our daily pursuit, we no longer worry about money because it comes to us when we need it. This past September I needed nineteen thousand dollars to conduct a business transaction, and I possessed a liquid amount of a little more than half of what I needed.

A good friend offered my wife and me nine thousand dollars to help us without even blinking. Let me be clear, a friend offered us $9,000 without us even asking. This, undoubtedly, was a testament to how she felt about us and an unspoken trust and confidence in what we were doing. More, specifically, that is God working in our lives. I am thankful to have friends like this not only in difficult times but at any time.

Today is Wednesday, October 23, and since April 5th, I've had various minor incidents that required immediate attention and money I didn't have at the time. However, payments for services showed up and credit cards with large credit lines appeared without the required credit application. In Napoleon Hill's famous book, *Think and Grow Rich*, he writes: "...You may as well know, right here, that you can never have riches in great quantities, unless you work yourself into a white heat of desire for money and, actually, believe you will possess it."[144]

Although the context of Hill's statement is focused directly on acquiring great sums of money, it reminds me of exactly what I believe faith is. If we don't have the "white hot desire" for what God has promised us, we don't really believe it and will not achieve it. It's amazing how a *spiritual* faith and belief forms the *material* substance of our lives, and it's comforting to know that God anointed the *path* before we were even born. The following quote applies to every expression of God including you.

"Before I formed you in the womb I knew you, and before you were born I consecrated you; I appointed you a prophet to the nations." (Jeremiah 1:5, ESV)[145]

---

[144] Napoleon Hill, *Think and Grow Rich (1937)*

[145] English Standard Version (ESV), Jeremiah 1:5

During preparation for my entrepreneurial journey, I registered my company with the state two years in advance of conducting full-time operations and opened a business checking account. I met with a few friends and family members to seek their affirmation and investments in my dream to show my bank that I had a solid business plan with both savings and outside investor income. This was based on the premise that I would need a business loan near the end of the first year, to sustain and grow operations large enough to earn the same income I was making in my current job.

Unfortunately, I was unable to achieve enough interest to attract outside investors. And even though I had more than $130,000 of personal savings and business purchases flowing through my checking account for over a year, my bank and several others denied my business credit applications.

With a "bullet-proof" business plan and not enough savings to maintain me and my family for the first year of operations, fear and doubt rushed through a slightly opened doorway with a muscular appearance and a "Cheshire grin." Even though I felt defeated, I yelled out *Psalms 23* with the commitment, confidence and appreciation required to show God I had the faith of this intention.

"1 The LORD is my shepherd, I lack nothing. 2He makes me lie down in green pastures, he leads me beside quiet waters, 3 he refreshes my soul. He guides me along the right paths for his name's sake. 4 Even though I walk through the darkest valley, I will fear no evil, for you are with me; your rod and your staff, they comfort me. 5 You prepare a table before me in the presence of my enemies. You anoint my head with oil; my cup overflows. 6 Surely your goodness and love will follow me all the days of my life, and I will dwell in the house of the LORD forever." (Psalms 23, NIV)[146]

Bob Hope once said, "a bank is a place that will lend you money if you can prove that you don't need it."[147] From my perspective he

---

[146] New International Version (NIV), Psalms 23,

[147] Bob Hope Quote http://www.brainyquote.com/quotes/quotes/b/bobhope161800.html

is exactly right! I feel banks are no longer relevant for nontraditional entrepreneurs and small businesses because the requirements are too steep for those of us who have average credit scores and meager assets. Even more so, if we could fulfill their loan application requirements, we wouldn't need the money. Yet without outside investors and bank loans, I've launched two businesses under the Pannell Enterprises LLC concept.

"For still the vision awaits its appointed time; it hastens to the end—it will not lie. If it seems slow, wait for it; it will surely come; it will not delay," (Habakkuk 2:3, ESV).[148]

Again money is not the first priority in our lives. We must prepare ourselves to attract money by developing the details of our idea and seeking guidance from God on the intent and purpose. Since money is a very important tool, however, we use it to advance the vision that was preinstalled in us for the Purpose of God. Therefore money is used as a means to accomplish the vision of our hearts and to support the commitments of those we are led to assist.

I'm fully aware that every person on their *path* comes to a place of sincere need at certain moments throughout their lifetime. I also believe that a measured part of our walk includes helping others to recognize God's Potential in their lives. As the *pendulum of equilibrium* for every person swings with periodic disruption and imbalance in our lives, I believe we will attract money and support with the same consistency and faithfulness that we have offered it. When we faithfully apply money to realizing the true idea, it comes as needed, and we never lack the appropriate means.

Bottom line: money is a piece of the puzzle, and when we have faithfully identified the pieces to assemble a clear vision of the idea, God offers access to the remaining pieces of the mystery.

---

[148] English Standard Version (ESV), Habakkuk 2:3

"I appeal to you, brothers, to watch out for those who cause divisions and create obstacles contrary to the doctrine that you have been taught; avoid them."– Romans 16:17 (ESV)

PART TEN
United We Stand

Today, my journey has brought me to Sunday, October 27, 2013, which is the start of the eleventh week, during my thirteen week *season*. God through the presence of the eternal Spirit has offered me grace, mercy and other gifts that have blossomed into delicious fruits by virtue of taking a walk on this *path*.

"But the fruit of the Spirit is love, joy, peace, longsuffering (patience), kindness, goodness, faithfulness, gentleness, self-control," (Galatians 5:22-23, NKJV).[149]

I no longer, frequently, entertain the shadows of fear and doubt that prevented me from stepping onto my *path* in the beginning, although they visit sometimes to question my progress. We will never escape fear, doubt, frustration, anger, or any other adverse emotional feeling that tests our soul, as we continue our physical journey. By nature we carry the potential of these emotions in the "fabric" of our bodies and ignoring them places us on an expressway to disastrous consequences. We must, consciously, acknowledge our emotions, daily,

---

[149] New King James Version (NKJV), Galatians 5:22-23

and observe the thoughts that charge them. Thoughts plus emotion equal feeling.

Hindsight always offers "20/20 vision" because we are able to view circumstances that are separate from our-*self*, as a spectator instead of a participant. From my vantage point on the *path*, since being charged with a DUI on June 2, 2012, there have been three primary event dates, which "tested" my resolve and the faith of my intentions. The first one occurred on June 2nd when I pledged to stop drinking, in order to identify the life changes I needed to make with a clear mind.

The second event was on April 5, 2013 when I left my "secure" career in the government to pursue my entrepreneurship dream of starting and running a company. I resigned my position with "the faith of a mustard seed" believing that God would lead me to the business clients I was unable to attract while working in my full-time career.[150] Pannell Enterprises LLC began with Food Vending Solutions as the first operating arm of the company on April 5th.

In *Part Five*, I spoke of an "experienced entrepreneur in his mid-70s," who coached me and supported my entry in the frozen food distribution industry. He introduced me to several industry professionals that I would've never met on my own and encouraged me all the way to my first clients.

With a target goal of obtaining two food vending machine placements by May, I obtained three vending placements by the 1st of June with the assistance of an, exceptionally, talented sales professional. Additionally, I invested in my first refrigerated trailer in July to transport cold and frozen foods and formed another business the very next month in August named Fridge On Wheels Rentals. God is Good all the time!

The third event happened surprisingly on Sunday, August 18, 2013. The experiences recorded in this journal were in response to listening to an "inner" voice that conveyed an inaudible message about meekness. I didn't ignore it and the pursuit became a major victory for

---

[150] New International Version (NIV), Matthew 17:20

me because I "freely" chose to identify the meaning of it in my life.

This is also, an example of the openness I've expressed throughout the journal that is critical for a "breakthrough" we may be expecting in our lives. It would be difficult to tie "meekness" to anything other than God, so we can evaluate epiphanies and feelings like these with good intent. I'm expecting to share this journal with others, who like me may be just one major decision away from discovering their dream.

We exist here as spirit in human form to rediscover and fulfill God's Purpose for our lives. Even though you may have once thought that God was far away and separate from us, hopefully, this journal has offered a fresh perspective for beginning a walk of self-discovery on your *path*. If you recognized content that "spoke" to you, the finding will not leave you alone until you, consciously, work to uncover the mystery. Once you've opened the box with a new puzzle piece, a new journey begins, and the new piece won't fit on your old puzzle board.

It's not stated every day, nor did I, truly, understand it before I began writing this journal, but Christianity is not a religion. Christianity is a "belief system" that offers the Power of God through faithful living. As it is written, Christianity, through the declaration of Jesus the Christ does not permit fear, doubt, guilt, and any other adverse emotional feelings to drive our lives, because they are obstacles to receiving the gifts on the *path* that we've chosen. It is also written that Jesus Christ walked among men to demonstrate the Love of the Father and to do Purposeful works through faith, as shown below.

5 "Lord," said Thomas, "we do not know where You are going, so how can we know the way?" 6 Jesus answered, "I am the way, and the truth, and the life. No one comes to the Father except through Me. 7 If you had known Me, you would know My Father as well. From now on you do know Him and have seen Him." 8 Philip said to Him, "Lord, show us the Father, and that will be enough for us." 9 Jesus replied, "Philip, I have been with you all this time, and still you do not know Me? Anyone who has seen Me has seen the Father. How can you say, 'Show us the Father'? 10 Do you not believe that I am in the Father and the Father is in Me? The words I say to you, I do not speak on My own. Instead, it is the Father dwelling in Me, performing His

works. [11]Believe Me that I am in the Father and the Father is in Me—or at least believe on account of the works themselves. [12]Truly, truly, I tell you, whoever believes in Me will also do the works that I am doing. He will do even greater things than these, because I am going to the Father. [13]And I will do whatever you ask in My name, so that the Father may be glorified in the Son. [14]If you ask Me anything in My name, I will do it."
(John 14:5-14, BSB) [151]

Righteous works require love and the faith of our intentions. *"Whoever pursues righteousness and love finds life, prosperity and honor."* (Proverbs 21:21, NIV).[152] Therefore, Jesus provides a paradigm for people of all faiths and religions, because His life examples reveal a personal relationship with the Creator and a commitment to Love and His Purpose. As I've expressed throughout, faith is not practiced by thinking. No matter how much we think we are faithful the results of our faith are shown in the outcomes of how our feelings and our dealings interact. My walk has taught me that faith is a "3-D" illustration of confidence, commitment, and appreciation for the stated belief with a "knowing" that God will fulfill His Promise.

With "tenured" dedication I've tried short-cuts, longer routes, and countless other ways and I've found no way around this. To get to the type of faith that drives purpose and meaning in our lives, consistently, we must observe a reliable balance among our *material* and *spiritual* dual nature. By His Design, we all have a natural tendency for certain moments, desires, experiences, and possessions to say the least. But our tallest vision is impossible to see if our *material* impulses are in the driver's seat, constantly. The Spirit offers the GPS with supreme guidance, as long as we accept it with joy and appreciation, which I've also heard is faith in action.

We must be, fully, open to God's Promise for our lives, or we will not see the goodness that awaits us. Christianity compels each person to discover his or her dream and obliges these faithful voyagers to "attract" others to show them the way through an *"agape"* or unconditional

---

[151] Berean Study Bible (BSB), John 14:5-14
[152] New International Version (NIV), Proverbs 21:21

131

love. Putting on the *The Armor of God* means that we are, faithfully, prepared to follow the *path to our inheritance* using the Power of God.

[10] "Finally, be strong in the Lord and in his mighty power. [11] Put on the full armor of God, so that you can take your stand against the devil's schemes. [12] For our struggle is not against flesh and blood, but against the rulers, against the authorities, against the powers of this dark world and against the spiritual forces of evil in the heavenly realms. [13] Therefore put on the full armor of God, so that when the day of evil comes, you may be able to stand your ground, and after you have done everything, to stand. [14] Stand firm then, with the belt of truth buckled around your waist, with the breastplate of righteousness in place, [15] and with your feet fitted with the readiness that comes from the gospel of peace. [16] In addition to all this, take up the shield of faith, with which you can extinguish all the flaming arrows of the evil one. [17] Take the helmet of salvation and the sword of the Spirit, which is the word of God. [18] And pray in the Spirit on all occasions with all kinds of prayers and requests. With this in mind, be alert and always keep on praying for all the Lord's people." (Ephesians 6:10-18, NIV)[153]

There is a, naturally, occurring condition for unity in our world, and Christianity prepares us for the walk if we are open to it. We are all individual expressions of the One Mind of God travelling together in the same direction toward Divine Perfection. Together we are the Body of Christ with its diverse nature and unique talents to honor God, in accordance with His Will and according to His Purpose.

[12] "Just as a body, though one, has many parts, but all its many parts form one body, so it is with Christ. [13] For we were all baptized by one Spirit so as to form one body—whether Jews or Gentiles, slave or free—and we were all given the one Spirit to drink. [14] Even so the body is not made up of one part but of many." (1 Corinthians 12:12-14, NIV)[154]

On my journey during this thirteen week season, I have come

---

[153] New International Version (NIV), Ephesians 6:10-18
[154] New International Version (NIV), 1 Corinthians 12:12-14

to one final conclusion. The *material* reality we live in only exists to worship and honor God by showing the Goodness and Power of God in our lives. I establish this perspective based on the English translations of ancient writings, Biblical scriptures, scientific discovery, and the recognized *spiritual* aspect of our dual nature.

God is Everything and All Things including ourselves. However, we have forgotten this as we journey in our current human form. I've tried to offer a clear and compelling case by way of the perceptual matters of my journey that faith is the only way to God's Goodness and we can only get there with a complete submission to His Will.

But faith is not what our thoughts tell us it is. It is shown by the "substance" of our lives, which blossoms like fruit, as a testament to the beauty of faith for others to inquire how we became so, "wonderfully made." Faith demotes logic for *material* purposes only and is fundamental for creating our lives, consciously.

Business opportunities continue to open up for me without me looking for them as they are attracted to my purpose. That's God! I'm merely an open "vessel" willing to receive these blessings. Before this journey, I didn't believe it was possible for openness to be the primary means by which faith operates.

Let's be "real," submission to God means we are open to turning the next page of our lives without hesitation. That's scary for those who believe they are in control of some-thing. We may control something, which is primarily our-*selves*. However, God controls everything, and I would rather be working for the Controller of All Things and Everything, rather than my-*self* or any other.

This journal is comprised of ten *Parts,* and I was led to the number 10 because ancient philosophy considered it to be a "perfect" number and representative of God. I believe I'm on a journey toward Perfection, but I may never see it in this life. I've learned to be okay with that. I believe the information written here is inspired by Truth, in a way that fulfills God's Promise for my life. From beginning to end I've included the assumptions I had, which are widely shared in society and often prohibit us from achieving our divine inheritance.

Contrary to popular belief, your responsibility to you and

everyone else in your life, is to rediscover your true purpose. The Divine Plan was established before we were born, and all we need to do is answer the call in our lives when the "the bell tolls for us."[155] We all know without caller ID when that call arrives. However, will we be aware at that moment or at subsequent ones to answer?

On earth and throughout the universe, we exist as interdependent organisms that depend on each other for survival in a Divine "hierarchy." This hierarchy does not exist according to importance but does so, in accordance with Purpose.

All things contribute to the Whole of Existence, and separation among us and all other things occurs based on the specific role we play in the process of exchange. Every person has a unique role to play in our world, individually, and these roles intersect with other "character" roles to manifest History of Love United on earth – God. It appears to me that Psalm 117, which is the shortest Psalm chapter in the Bible may offer the Purpose of Unity among all people on earth. All people exist to worship and praise God.

[1] "Praise the LORD, all you nations; extol him, all you peoples. [2] For great is his love toward us, and the faithfulness of the LORD endures forever. Praise the LORD."[156]

At this point of our journey together, there should be no surprise or controversy about the findings here. I find the evidence offered here to be persuasive about the Purpose of our existence based on: 1) my observations during the walk on my *path* this season, 2) the Bible and other ancient literature, and 3) some of the latest discoveries in science that tie these distinct components together with a ribbon.

These "3-D" observations demonstrate an exceptional consistency that is difficult to ignore. I hope my perspectives and ideas inspire others to step on their *paths*. When we have, fully, contemplated, prayed and meditated on the intent of the "inner" idea, and the vision of what that

---

[155] No Man Is An Island Quotes http://www.goodreads.com/work/quotes/6791114-no-man-is-an-island

[156] New International Version (NIV) Psalm 117

intent looks like, we are able to manifest the *material* confidence and *spiritual* faith to wear the Amor of God. I believe the Purpose of Life is to learn who we are and to journey with God to the place He has prepared just for us. We walk this *path* with meek strength.

"Let not your heart be troubled; you believe in God, believe also in Me. ² In My Father's house are many mansions; if it were not so, I would have told you. I go to prepare a place for you. ³ And if I go and prepare a place for you, I will come again and receive you to Myself; that where I am, there you may be also. ⁴ And where I go you know, and the way you know." (John 14:1-4, NKJV)[157]

"There is neither Jew nor Greek, there is neither slave nor free, there is neither male nor female; for you are all one in Christ Jesus" (Galatians 3:28, NKJV).[158]

Bottom line: the expression of God's Potential is incomplete, until we are, consciously, aware of who we are, individually, and attract others to walk the Divine Path according to His Purpose.

Did my season reveal God's Promise?

"Blessed is the one who perseveres under trial because, having stood the test, that person will receive the crown of life that the Lord has promised to those who love him." (James 1:12 NIV)

There is more to my story for inspired souls that is impossible to believe without understanding what you, previously, read. If you agree with the premise of Meek Strength and would like to examine the results of my season, and explore the potential of this fresh approach in relationship to your personal vision, please go to my author page at www.ianpannell.author.

---

[157] New King James Version (NKJV), John 14:1-4
[158] New King James Version (NKJV), Galatians 3:28,

CPSIA information can be obtained
at www.ICGtesting.com
Printed in the USA
BVHW041132150620
581563BV00005B/19

9 781952 617584